Compass Quests

The Black Stone

Rachel Hurbon

MILTON & HUGO L.L.C.
4407 Park Ave., Suite 5
Union City, NJ 07087, USA

Website: *www.miltonandhugo.com*
Hotline: *1-888-778-0033*
Email: *info@miltonandhugo.com*

Ordering Information:
Quantity sales. Special discounts are granted to corporations, associations, and other organizations. For more information on these discounts, please reach out to the publisher using the contact information provided above.

Library of Congress Control Number:		2024916505	
ISBN-13:	979-8-89285-182-4	[Paperback Edition]	
	979-8-89285-183-1	[Hardback Edition]	
	979-8-89285-181-7	[Digital Edition]	

Rev. date: 08/08/2024

CHAPTER

— 1 —

"Annabell, what were you thinking?" I muttered to myself, frustrated. I climbed the stairs to the second-floor landing. I was going to the study. On a Saturday. I went in there only for tutoring and nothing more. But why was I going there today? Because I had left my Bible there. I chastised myself. I brought it with me everywhere, and somehow I managed to forget it the other day during lessons.

I entered the room, looking around hastily. School was not my favorite thing, and I wanted to get my Bible and leave. If my tutor was there, it could have been worse: he would have tried to give me a side lesson if he saw me. I glanced around again. My tutor was not there.

I looked around the room for a minute and then found my Bible. It was where I had left it, on the book stand next to the world atlas. I quickly grabbed it and left the room. I let out a sigh of relief as I rushed down the hall. I went to my bedroom, and closed the door.

My room was in the upper parts of the castle near the library. As a result, I had developed a liking for reading. Our library was one of the biggest rooms in the castle, save the grand hall and the ballroom. I sat down on my bed and gingerly rubbed the leather cover of the Bible, cracked and worn from use. Oh, how I loved the wisdom it gave. Usually, on Saturdays, I spent most of my time reading my Bible or other books. It was one of my favorite things, and Saturday was the best time to do it, as I had no lessons.

As a princess, it was a relief to have the library near my room. It would allow me, for a few minutes out of the day, to escape to another place and let my mind travel through the world of the story I was reading. I had read hundreds of books. Each of them had given me some sort of feeling—some causing laughter, others causing tears. But only my Bible was the one book that truly made me feel safe and gave me peace when I most needed it.

Stroking its cover again, I opened it up to where I had left off. I was in the book of Psalms, chapter 13. I read the Psalm and came to the last two verses: "But I will trust in your unfailing love; My heart rejoices in your salvation. I will sing the Lord's praise, for he has been good to me." I sighed in contentment and gazed at the wall. Those verses were true. I could always trust God and thank Him through praise, even if I couldn't see the outcome yet. I smiled at the thought.

There was a knock on my door. I glanced toward it. "Come in."

Hanna, one of the maids, opened the door and walked in. She stopped, apologetically, when she saw the open Bible on my lap.

"Oh, Your Highness, I'm sorry. I didn't mean to interrupt."

I let out a disappointed sigh. It looked as though I wouldn't be getting much reading done today. I could tell she had something to tell me. I marked the page I was on, closed the Bible, and set it on the shelf where I normally kept it.

I turned to Hanna and asked, "That's all right. What is it you would like to tell me?"

Hanna's face lit up. "Their Majesties have returned from the Central Continent."

I gasped with delight and rushed past her and out of the room. My parents had been traveling for almost a month now. They had gone on a political trip with the kings and queens of the other continents. There had been some disagreements and difficulties between the continents, as there were tensions between them. Each of the continents—North, East, South, West, and Central—were all a part of a landmass called the Compass. The kings and the queens of each continent met at the Central continent to resolve matters. My parents coming home meant they had been successful.

"Annabell! My lady!"

Hanna ran after me as I charged down the stairs. I was too excited to wait. After all, I hadn't seen my parents in what felt like forever. When I reached ground level, I picked up my skirts and ran faster. I passed a window and caught a glimpse of the royal carriage. Hanna was still calling after me to slow down, but I ignored her.

Reaching the grand hall, I rushed to the large double doors. I was so glad that my parents had returned that I pushed the doors open harder than I should have. They flew open and hit the walls outside with a bang. My father was already out of the carriage talking with my mother. He glanced up at the noise and saw me running through the courtyard.

"My darling Annabell!" he called out, a smile spreading across his face. When I reached them, Father caught me in a hug and swung me around. My father was a tall man. Being forty-five years old, his brown hair and beard now had streaks of gray in them. His favorite color was emerald green, and he wore it nearly every day. Today he had on a green embroidered tunic with a lighter-green overcoat.

"There you are, dear. We were wondering where you were." My Mother, Queen Casia, beamed as I danced with Father.

I smiled at her in reply as I tried to stay focused on the dance steps that Father was completing in rapid succession. It was a tradition that Father had shared with me since I was three. Whenever he was away for a while, he would come find me, and then we would dance. My mother stood there watching us with her amused smile, which was what she usually did when she found us dancing together. She always managed to wear the same color green as Father, but it always looked different, as though she hadn't worn the same color green the day before. Her brown hair was always done in a neat bun decorated with a green ribbon. Father stopped dancing and released me from his grip. He was out of breath.

"You've gotten better at that. I can't keep up with you anymore." He sat on the carriage step to catch his breath.

I hugged my parents. "I've missed you."

My mother nodded. "As have we. But come, let us go inside. I hope to see everything as we left it."

Walking forward, she gave Father a sly sidelong glance and then went to give me a playful shove on the shoulder. I dodged her hand, laughing, and fell into step with her. She had left me in charge while they were away. I was proud to say that nothing had gone awry. Father stood and caught up to us.

"Oh, I am sure she did a marvelous job, Casia. No need to worry. I say let's go to the dining hall for dinner."

Mother laughed as Father exaggerated the motion to escort her to the hall. "Oh, Harold! Please try to at least have some dignity."

Father led her to the hall, and I followed, smiling. I hoped that they would be staying for a while longer than usual. My parents traveled a lot on political business. Those recent skirmishes between the continents had kept them away for months. I was glad they were back because they had made it in time for my fourteenth birthday.

In the summer of my fifteenth year, the sun shone through the study window. My tutor, Sir Warren, was teaching me about something in the history of Misby, but I wasn't paying attention. I was thinking about the upcoming summer. There was so much that I wanted to do with my parents. I was hoping that they wouldn't have to travel as much this year. I was often lonely, even with the library and my Bible. Sir Warren was still rambling on. He was a tall and thin man, and his long robe made him look thinner. The professor's curly black hair was combed neatly around the professor's cap that he always wore.

History, the last lesson of the day, always felt the longest. It was true, he did teach with enthusiasm, but his voice was boring. As a princess of one of the three kingdoms on the Northern Continent, I was expected to learn all about history. Half of the time, though, I wasn't interested. Sir Warren stopped his explanatory pace and tapped me on the shoulder.

"Your Highness? I understand that this is the last day of your studies, but you must pay attention."

I sighed. No matter how hard he tried, Sir Warren was not a fun tutor. He lectured more than anything else.

Sometimes I think he just liked to hear himself talk. About an hour later after a long lecture on how Misby came to be, he excused me from the study. The study was in an upper room of the castle. It was a fair-sized room built in an *L* shape. A large window on one of the walls let in the light. The room had an entire section of books on another wall that had been taken from the library. It was not far from the library and my room. Just outside of the study entrance was a long corridor that was lined with windows that let in the light and summer sun.

As I walked down the hallway to my room, I looked out the windows I passed. They were just above the outer wall, and I could see the surrounding mountains that Misby sat in. I had always loved being outdoors and would spend some time outside whenever I got a chance. In the past, I would stand on the outer wall, and the wind would sweep over me and off the edge, taking my worries and concerns with it, completely setting me free.

I sighed as I continued making my way down the hall. The subjects that I was learning were not at all interesting. All my lessons were meant to prepare me for becoming the next ruler of Misby: history, government, social etiquette, and literature. They were just *fine* and *dandy* in and of themselves, but they were tedious to sit through. Putting one of my many history books away, I turned to

read some more of my Bible. Christianity was widely practiced on the Northern Continent, along with the others. It was particularly strong in Misby. I had just turned around again to leave and read in the library when I nearly ran into Phillip. I jumped, startled that he had just appeared.

"Oh, goodness! Why don't you ever knock?"

Philip was a page, but he was mostly used as a messenger in the castle. He was a young man of fifteen, with brown hair that he could never comb straight. He always wore the same type of clothing: a dark green shirt, brown pants, and a light-brown belt. He never said "Your Highness," but it somehow didn't seem to matter. His swiftness to deliver the message was amazing, but his stealth was another problem. He would often pop up out of nowhere without anyone noticing. He also had a habit of coming into a room without knocking, but he had a fascinating talent for coming in without being heard.

"Your Father, King Herold, wants to see you. He is out waiting in the courtyard," he said hurriedly and then left.

Oh dear, I thought. Father sent Phillip only if something was important. And Phillip always delivered Father's messages hurriedly if they were concerning me. Why he did this, I had no idea, but it was always a sure sign that something was going to happen. I returned my Bible to its shelf and then hurried out of the room and into the courtyard. It was not too far from my room and only a stairway down. On my way down the stairs, I passed Mother and Father's room. It was quite large, with a four-poster bed and a fireplace. It was almost large enough to be the size of the grand hall. A large coat of arms hung on the headboard. It was decorated with three mountains and Tirellian filigree, a type of gem found in the surrounding mountains. The walls were painted a forest green, making the room a little dark.

Three maids were in the room, and they were packing one of my parents' large traveling trunks. More specifically, my Mother's. I paused to consider going into the room, but then brushed it off as I continued down the stairs. Seeing them pack meant only one thing. I quickened my pace through the grand hall, my footsteps echoing off the arched pillars and walls. When I reached the courtyard, I saw Father and Mother standing in front of the royal carriage talking to each other.

I groaned. I had been right. My parents were traveling again even though they had just gotten back two days ago. The carriage meant that they were traveling somewhere that I couldn't go. I was hardly ever allowed to go with them because I was their only heir or something like that. But why did they have to travel so much? I let out a sigh, rubbing the back of my neck in disappointment as I approached them.

Father looked up and gave a comforting smile.

"Ah, Annabell. There you are. Your mother and I are going to Appline. Her cousin is getting married, and he invited us—"

"But not me," I said, finishing his sentence with a sigh. He nodded, giving me a sympathetic look. I glanced at both of them.

"Are you sure I can't come with you? Is it that I'm too young?"

Mother shook her head and gently laid her hand on my shoulder

"No, darling. You're fifteen—you are old enough to attend. It's just he didn't say anything about you in the invitation."

I raised my eyebrows in surprise

"That's ridiculous! I'm a part of his extended family—shouldn't I be able to come?"

Mother gave me a look at my outburst, and Father laid a hand on her shoulder

"Well … technically, yes. You should be able to come, but when your mother and I sent him a message to change his mind, he was firmly against it."

"Why?"

"We don't know. It's not like Charles to exclude family members, but I'm sure he has a good reason." Mother's face softened again as I nodded and let out a frustrated sigh. She pulled me closer to her, and I fell into her arms, fighting back the urge to cry.

"I know you don't like it when we travel, Annabell, and I know it's hard to try and stay occupied when you are by yourself." She tilted my head up to look at her. "Believe me, I know … Just remember for me that even when you feel alone, or scared, or worried, you must lean into God and go to him for help and peace. All right?"

I nodded in response. "I love you. Come back soon."

"We will, darling. I love you too," Mother said quietly, resting her cheek on the top of my head while she stroked my hair. She released me and got into the carriage. Father hugged me and gently cupped my face in his hands.

"I love you, Annabell. We'll see you in two weeks. Okay?"

I nodded, the urge to cry fading. "Okay."

Father got into the carriage. The driver called out to the horses, and the carriage surged forward and out of the courtyard, fading out of sight into the gathering fog. I sent up a prayer for their protection, as the sight of them disappearing in the gloom felt like a warning.

"Your Majesty, where are you going?" a voice called out in a condescending tone across the courtyard.

I growled in my throat. It was Father's advisor, Renon. I disliked him so much. He was a tall, thin man just like Father. His mustache was pencil-thin as well, and his beard covered only his chin. He *always* wore a red robe and tunic with a gold embroidered sash. His face was very thin, deepening any expression he made. He frowned a lot, making his company unpleasant to everyone but my father. I liked to call him a master frowner in my head. Along with the advisor chain, the crest of Misby stamped into a silver pendant, he also had a small glass ball around his neck. It was hardly noticeable, but when you did see it, it made his outfit look incomplete.

Not only did I dislike his appearance, but I detested how he treated me whenever Father and Mother were not around, which was quite frequent. His responses were rude, and he called me "Your Majesty" in a way that made it seem unimportant and sarcastic. He always tried to prevent me from doing something. What was worse was that he wasn't a believer in Christ. He made things hard for others who were. I was constantly praying that he would be changed and that God would help me with my attitude toward him.

"Nothing. Please stop worrying."

I sighed. I was actually on my way to the castle wall. I usually spent my time up there when my parents were away. I climbed the steps and looked over the battlement. Our kingdom, Misby, was in the mountain range, the Falls, on the Northern Continent. There were only five continents in the whole world. Four of the land masses, the Northern Continent, the Eastern Continent, the Southern Continent, and the Western continent, had been formed roughly like arrowheads. The Central Continent, the one my parents had traveled to a year earlier, was in a rough square.

Misby was only one of the three kingdoms that ruled the Northern Continent. Its capital was established in the middle of a large valley to protect it from the other two kingdoms. From my geography lesson, I tried to remember where the Kingdom of Appline was. It was the closest kingdom to the tip of the continent. I thought about my parents, wondering how far they were on their travels. It had been three days since they left, and I was already bored and lonely. By now they should have been at least halfway there.

Bong! Bong! Bong!

The alarm rang out from the nearest guard tower, making me jump.

"Griffin! Griffin sighted!" Vigilate, the guard in the tower, called frantically to the others in the courtyard. He rang the bell so furiously I thought his armor would come flying off. Guards rushed to and fro on the wall and in the courtyard. The servants rushed inside as I glanced up at the sky. A large gold Griffin was flying overhead. Just as its shadow passed over me, Renon was suddenly there, pulling me down the stairs. How did he always manage to show up right when something was happening?

"Let go of me!" I commanded, trying to pull my wrist out of his hand.

His grip didn't loosen. He looked up once or twice as the Griffin circled overhead. He seemed annoyed. He took me to the grand hall and shoved me inside. He hurriedly closed the door just as the Griffin landed and stood leaning against them. I caught a glimpse of its gold feathers as the doors shut. I glared at him, annoyed.

"Why did you take me inside?"

"You know that Griffins are dangerous, Your Majesty," he said, huffing. His face was scrunched up in displeasure. There was clearly something about this that bothered him. This was also the first time that he had taken me inside to protect me. I glared at him suspiciously.

"It's a *Golden* Griffin! Not a clay one!" I yelled.

Trying to prevent me from going, he leaned harder on the doors. With a bit of struggle, I pushed him off and stormed out of the hall. Griffins were one of the animals that lived in the valley. Their eagle's head had the feathers of a great horned owls. Their lion bodies had gigantic, feathered wings, and they had lion paws for their front and back legs. There were actually three Griffin species in our valley: golds, browns, and clays.

The clays and browns were wild and dangerous. Oftentimes, they were born with messed-up brown feathers and fur. In the past years, there had been a few village attacks from the clays and browns. Many of the villagers were terrified of them. The golds, on the other hand, were tame and the color of lion's fur. I was not frightened of Griffins like most girls my age might be. When I was little, I discovered that I could talk to them and other creatures. I smiled inwardly at the thought …

"Annabell? Darling? What are you doing?" I looked at Mother from my position on the ground.

"Just drawing, Momma." My pudgy little hands were holding two feather pens. Mother had laughed.

"You only need one to draw, dear. Here, let me go put this one back in the library." She took the pen from my hand and then left the room.

I turned my attention back to the page and the doodles I had been doing. It was meant to be a Griffin, but it didn't look like one whatsoever. I stood up, leaving my drawing to dry, and walked over to the window. I was too short to look out, so I kept a stool under the windowsill. As I climbed up, I leaned out, feeling the wind, and a moment later, I heard the beating of wings. I glanced up and saw a gold Griffin flying in a slow spiral downward. I squealed in delight. I had never seen a Griffin until now. My squeal caught its attention, and it swooped by.

"Hello!" I called as it came near.

"Hello young one!" it squawked. Then in the next second, it was gone.

"Did you say something, Annabell?"

I spun around. Mother was in the doorway. I hopped off the stool and ran to her.

"Did you hear him, Mamma?"

Mother had frowned. She thought I was making up a story. So although I had bounced with excitement that day, I promised myself not to tell anyone what I could do. It was the only secret I had from my parents.

My thoughts returned to the present as a guard came sliding up to my feet. I leaped back. Out in the courtyard, it was total chaos. The guards were attacking the Griffin. Lunging, dodging, trying to tie it down. The Griffin was also attacking, but it just seemed to be trying to get around the guards. It was muttering to itself.

"Why does one form make so much of a difference? Stop!" It swiped at a guard near its front paws.

"Guards! Please, stop!" I called out as I dodged another guard. I made my way out into the courtyard.

Fedren, the captain of the army, saw me and shouted to his men. "Stand down!" He held up his hand, and everything came to a halt.

The Griffin froze and stared at me, its blue eyes sparkling with familiarity. I stared at the Griffin for a second and then turned my attention to Capitan Fedren as he spoke.

"Your Majesty, you should be inside. Let us take care of this. What would I tell the king if you got injured while I or my men stood by?" Fedren was a middle aged man and was about a foot taller than me. He never wore all of his armor unless he had to. His green eyes contrasted with his dark-brown hair. He looked at me expectantly when I didn't move. I furrowed my brow slightly and gently clasped my hands together.

"Thank you, Captain, but you can obviously see that it's a Golden Griffin. It should not cause any harm."

A guard off to my right let out a snort.

"Unless you attack it," I added, almost glaring at him. "I would like to handle this."

Fedren eyed me suspiciously. I was known around the castle for being capable of handling almost any animal problem. A week ago, I actually got rats to leave the storerooms near the kitchen. I could tell this was a different matter entirely to Fedren, but it wasn't for me. I ignored his glance and turned to address all the guards.

"Please, stand down. Step back so I can try to coax this Griffin to leave."

Some of the guards began muttering, others just glanced around and started to drift away. Fedren stayed a few feet away from the Griffin. He wasn't going to move. The Griffin stared at me again with a shocked expression. Its golden brown feathers sparkled in the sun. The guards dispersed, but some still lingered in case of danger.

The Griffin blinked. "How?" it muttered.

I was confused. The voice sounded familiar. I was no more than three steps away from its front feet. Its head was at Fedren's height.

"It's okay," I whispered, not wanting Fedren to hear me. I slowly walked up to it, holding out my hand to show that I had nothing to harm it.

The Griffin's eyes flashed again. Frustration, fear, and despair rippled across its body. It sat on its haunches and lowered its head. It began to cry, its whole body convulsing with each sob.

"It's okay," I said again and laid my hands on the sides of its face and began stroking it. Its crying lessened, and it spoke.

"Annabell."

I stopped. I looked at it. That voice again. I knew it, but I was still confused.

"How … how do you know me?"

"My dearest daughter."

The tears finally reached their limit and trickled out of its eyes. I leaned close to the Griffin's face, and my mind made the connection. My father's brilliant sparkling blue eyes shone back at me. I stared out of shock and fear as my hands rested on his face.

"Father?"

CHAPTER

—2—

Father didn't nod—he just sat there, his whole body sagging, his Griffin head lowering further still. My hands slowly slid from his face in fear and despair

"What happened?"

His tears still flowed, but they came less often. He took a breath and then began.

"Your mother and I were only a day and a half away …

"Harold, what do you think will happen while we are gone?"

There was the slightest tone of worry in Queen Casia's voice. King Harold laid his hands on his wife's lap and gave her a smile.

"I am sure everything will be fine. Annabell has done well without us there."

The carriage suddenly came to a stop, and they both slid forward in their seats in surprise. Harold leaned out the window and called out to the driver.

"What are we stopping for?"

"The horses won't budge. They've stopped, and we can't get them to move."

It was indeed true. The second driver had gotten down and was trying to pull the horses forward. King Harold pulled his head back inside. The moment he did, the side of the carriage burst into flame. The horses screamed and suddenly dashed forward. The driver fell off with a fearful yell. The carriage rushed forward, and the beam that connected the horses to the carriage snapped. The beam hit the ground. A loud grinding sound echoed through the carriage.

"Harold!" Casia screamed. The carriage continued its mad rush and began to fall on its side. Harold grabbed hold of his wife and rammed his side into the burning door. They leaped out just as the carriage crashed onto its side. Harold and Casia stood staring at the burning wood, holding each other. The two drivers were nowhere to be seen, and the horses were long gone.

"Are you all right, dear?" Harold focused his attention on his wife. She was shaking.

"I … I don't know."

"Let me know if—Casia!" he yelled.

A red mist began to rise from the ground. He had let go of his wife for a second, and now he couldn't see her. A wind began sweeping around him. Sand seemed to be hitting him all over.

"Harold!" she screamed.

The mist spread. Thickening. Darkening. Sand kept flying. A barrier formed between the king and his queen.

"Casia! Where are you?"

Then just as suddenly as the mist and the wind appeared, it stopped. Harold shook his head to clear it. He looked up and nearly yelled. A Gold Griffin stood in front of him. He would have walked away had it not …

"Harold! Where are you?" the Griffin called out. Harold froze. The Griffin was looking around frantically. He looked down at his hands. They had become lion paws. He turned his head. A lion's body adorned with wings. He stared at his wife in shock. They had become

Griffins. Casia hadn't moved from her spot, but she was still searching for him in human form. Her sleek golden body trembled in fear. The wings that adorned her back shook with each cry. Harold was about to call out to her when a noise off to their right caught their attention.

Men in brown garb leaped out from the side of the path. Dozens of them came pouring out of the forest on either side of the road. Casia screamed. A net suddenly dropped from nowhere, and Harold let out a cry of rage as it fell on top of them. He clawed at the net and began to tear a hole. The men, whoever they were, began to throw another net on. Harold worked his way out of the first net and into safety just as the second net dropped. The attackers tried to tie him down, but he took off into the air.

Casia was still in the nets. She struggled and kicked and called out for Harold to help her. When he gained enough height in the air, he turned to help his wife. Just as he dived, a liquid was dumped onto the net by the men. Casia collapsed and a thick cloud of red smoke shot up into Harold's path. He quickly changed his course and circled back around. When the smoke cleared, his wife and their attackers were gone. He hovered in midair.

"Oh Lord ... Help me. Please."

Father sat there and then glanced up at me. I gasped for air. This was almost too much for me. Transformations. Griffins. Mother gone. I swallowed back a sob.

Father saw my distress and continued, "I came back here to get you. I don't want anything happening to you, and we need ..." He trailed off

"We need to go find Mother?" I whispered to him. I could feel that he was about to cry.

He nodded. I hugged his face to prevent myself from crying as well and whispered, "Oh, by all means, yes! Of course I'll come!"

I turned to Fedren. Releasing my father, I tried to compose myself.

"I am going to take a short trip. I ..." I paused, trying to think of what to say without it sounding strange.

"I need to go with this Griffin. I believe it wants me to go help—"

I was cut off by a crash. The doors to the grand hall were thrust open, and Renon, taking large, unhappy strides, rushed out.

"Your Majesty, I strongly advise against leaving. It would not be safe for you to travel alone, especially with your parents gone," he said, giving me the sharpest glare I had seen from anyone. He glanced at Father and scowled.

"I don't care, Renon. Besides, you're not my adviser. You're my father's." I crossed my arms and glared right back at him. It was extremely hard to do since he was a good foot taller than me. Fedren gave me a curious look at me for my explanation for leaving but didn't speak until now.

"I'm afraid I agree with Renon, Your Majesty."

I turned to him as I felt Father straighten up next to me. I could almost feel his anger.

"Fedren, I need to do this. I have to."

Fedren gently shook his head, sighing, and looked at me. "You're not going to stay even if I try to keep you here, are you?"

I shook my head, putting my hands on my hips in a defiant stance. He looked over at Father again. "I suppose ..."

Renon turned his glare to Fedren, seething, and Fedren hurried on. "If you insist on going, Your Majesty, you need someone to go with you."

Renon snorted in disapproval. Fedren glanced at Renon and then at me. He looked uncomfortable under Renon's cold stare.

"Please, take a guard."

I sighed. "Fine. I'll have Garen come with me. Tell him to meet me here tomorrow morning." I gave Father a reassuring glance and then spun on my heel and walked back into the castle.

It was the next morning, and the sun was just coming up over the mountains. I was in my room packing for the trip. I had put on my traveling dress and shoes, which I hardly ever wore. My padded traveling shoes were more comfortable to walk around in than my slippers. But I was too concerned about Mother to notice these things, though. My thoughts kept going back to her as I packed as quickly as possible. Where was she? Was she all right? Who had taken her, and where did they go? These thoughts kept circulating through my mind as I continued to pack. I glanced around the room, hoping I hadn't forgotten anything.

William, my pet great horned owl, was sitting there on his perch in the corner. He was watching me with his head cocked and his eyes slightly glazed over, as though he was thinking hard about something. I never liked it when he did that. I put my last pair of clothes in my satchel and headed out the door. I was crossing the grand hall and too caught up in my own thoughts when I ran straight into Garen.

"Ahhh!" I yelled as I bounced off him and fell to the ground.

"Oh! Sorry, Your Highness!" he said as he helped me off the floor.

Garen was one of the younger guards. He was twenty-seven years old and tall. His brown hair swooped over his forehead in wispy bangs. Garen often traveled with Mother and Father on their trips. Luckily for him, he didn't accompany them this time due to the fact that his mother needed assistance moving to a new home and he had been given time to do so.

Garen would often come and talk to me after his trips with Mother and Father and tell me what happened. He wasn't wearing his full armor, but he had on his breastplate and his sword as well. Another reason I liked him was because he never called me "Your Majesty," and I hated it when others did. I didn't want to be considered the ruler until I actually became queen. Garen picked my satchel up off the floor and, after dusting it off, handed it back to me.

"I wasn't looking where I was going," he said sheepishly.

"It's fine. I wasn't looking either," I said, brushing myself off and taking my satchel from him. I headed toward the doors of the hall, and he followed me out into the courtyard.

"Thank you for being willing to come with me. I know that this trip is unexpected, but it's really important."

Garen waved his hand. "Oh, I am glad to. I haven't been on a trip with Your Highness or your parents in a while."

I gave him a grateful glance and looked around the courtyard. Father was sitting down and being watched by a frightened guard.

"Good morning," he said. Raising one of his paws, he went to rub it over his face in exhaustion but found he couldn't. He let out a frustrated grunt and slammed his paw down again. The guard watched all of this with trepidation; he jumped and almost drew his sword when Father grunted.

I called out to him. "Don't! He's not going to do anything. He won't hurt you."

The guard nodded and released his hand from the hilt of the sword. Father cocked his head and gave me a questioning look. I walked up to him and rested my hands on the side of his face.

"Morning," I whispered to him.

I glanced around. Garen had dismissed the other guard and was watching nearby. We were alone in the courtyard. I turned my attention back to Father.

"Father … I know I never told you this before, but I can talk to you only because … well, when I was younger I found I could talk to Griffins and other … things." He stared at me, but the questioning look faded. He nodded his head slowly and then looked at me again.

"Listen," Father whispered to me, "you and Garen are going to ride me. It will be the quickest way to reach the carriage."

The night before, I had sneaked back into the courtyard, and Father and I discussed that if there was any way to find Mother, we should start at the carriage wreckage. Maybe I could catch a detail that he had missed. I nodded and turned to Garen, who was looking back at the grand hall doors as though something had caught his attention.

"Garen?"

"Hmm. Oh yes, Your Highness? I'm sorry. I thought I heard someone in the grand hall," he said as he turned toward me.

Father stood up, and Garen watched him rise. I gently patted Father's shoulder.

"We're going to ride on the Griffin to travel faster."

Garen suddenly looked worried. His body seemed to freeze. He swallowed and then asked quickly, "We're going to *ride* him?"

I stared at him, nonplussed by his response.

"Wait," I said, holding up my hands, "are you telling me that … you're scared of *heights?*"

He nodded, suddenly embarrassed. I blinked. He had told me almost everything about himself when we talked, but he never told me this. I was shocked. "I'm sorry to hear that. I didn't know."

He just shrugged.

"You must understand, though … this is the quickest way to travel."

He nodded again. Father crouched, chuckling softly, and Garen helped me climb up in between Father's wings. I sat between Father's shoulders, and Garen swung up after me. He didn't quite make it up, and he grabbed on to Father's fur for balance. Father grimaced in pain, and Garen closed his eyes tightly.

"Okay. I'm ready," he mumbled, and Father took off into the sky. Garen yelped at the sudden pull backward. I nearly lost my grip. Wind pulled at my cloak and my hair. A wide smile burst across my face as we leveled out and shot through a cloud.

21

Some hours later, I still thought flying was amazing. The wind whipped my cloak's hood off my head and pulled some of my strawberry blond hair out of its braid. I would probably have had more fun if I had not been so concerned about Mother. We passed another cloud. I leaned forward to talk to Father.

"How much farther is it?" I turned to look at Garen and noticed with alarm that his eyes were shut tight and his face was pale. He looked about ready to fall off.

"I don't think Garen can take much more of this," I yelled to be heard over the wind.

"Not much farther," Father replied. "Tell him to hang on just a little while longer."

Soon he started spiraling downward. The carriage wreckage was right below us. The air grew warmer, and I shivered at the temperature change. When we landed, Garen fell off Father's back and collapsed face down on the ground.

"Oh, the ground. How wonderful," he said, his voice muffled.

I held back a laugh and got off my father's back. I slid off and managed to stay standing up. After helping Garen up, I looked around. Eyes wide, I had to hold back a cry of fear. There in front of us was my father's carriage. The atmosphere made the scene look worse. Tall trees that lined the road blocked most of the afternoon sun, making the area extremely shaded. One of the carriage's wheel was broken, and it was off the dirt road, lying on its side in the grassy ditch. It lay on its side with another wheel in the air. The door lay in pieces on the ground, charred.

I walked up to the carriage. On its side, it reached the top of my shoulders. I set my hands on the edge and pushed myself up. There was a ring of blackened wood around the door. Other than that, the carriage was completely unburned. The doorway was the only charred section.

"That's weird," I said. I gently laid my hand on the burned section and sat there thinking.

"Um, not to be rude, but why are we here?" Garen asked. He had come up to the carriage and was looking at the burned section. He was right next to my shoulder. I stiffened, surprised at his sudden closeness. I wrestled with whether or not I should tell him about Father and what I could do. While I debated, Father came and stood next to Garen.

Garen shifted to his left, giving Father space, and swallowed nervously. I turned to him, still sitting on the carriage's side.

"Listen, there's something you should know about me. I … I can talk to creatures and other things."

He looked at me quizzically. I continued, feeling embarrassed. "That's why we're here. I found out that that's my father. When you heard squawking and clacking, I heard Father," I said, pointing to the Griffin.

Garen's eyes widened, and then he pointed to Father.

"*That's* King Herold?"

When I nodded, he turned to Father. "Oh, Your Majesty! I'm sorry! I didn't recognize that it was you."

Father sounded amused as he replied, "It's fine."

"What did he say?" Garen asked.

"He said it's okay," I said, looking back at the carriage door.

"How long have you been able to do this?" Both of them asked me at the same time.

"Since I was little." I looked from the door to the ground and then to Garen. "Wait. Garen, can you come stand by the door?"

I carefully climbed down, and Garen stood where the door would have been if the carriage was upright.

"Now, Father, you said you and Mother leaped out, right?"

He nodded.

"All right, then. Now, Garen, take the biggest step you can manage." I went and stood back from Garen and out of his way.

He mimicked the leap by putting one foot as far forward as he could manage. As his boot came down, the smallest, most unnoticeable stone turned black.

23

"Oh! Pull your foot back, quick!" I yelled and rushed forward to make sure he wouldn't fall forward.

Garen returned to his normal position. The stone had turned gray again. I knelt down close to the stone, close enough to where it didn't change color again. It didn't look any different than the others around it. I needed someone to examine it to answer a question that came into my mind, but I didn't want to touch it. It could do something to me that I might not have wanted.

"What is it?" Garen and Father asked at the same time as I picked up the pebble in a handkerchief that I had gotten from my satchel.

"Well," I began, standing up, "when the carriage caught on fire, Father said that he and Mother leaped out. Garen, your largest step would have been a leap for Father."

"So?" Father said, sounding a little annoyed that I didn't come right out with what I was thinking.

I continued, hoping that he would understand, "So what I'm saying is that magic was used to get you and Mother out of the carriage. A spell must have been set so that when you reached a certain place, the horses would stop and a fire would start. The fire was meant to get you out of the carriage. That's why only the area around the door burned."

I walked over to the fallen carriage and pointed to the broken wheel. "The wheel must have also been planned to break to cause the carriage to tip right where the stone was placed. The crash would have given the bandits, or whoever they were, enough time to throw the nets. As you ran from the carriage, you must have gotten near enough to touch this." I held up the stone, which remained gray.

"This is what turned you and Mother into Griffins. It was placed there purposely so that you would change. I've never seen or heard of anything that can do this. So now the question I have is, who made it … and why would they want you to transform?"

24

CHAPTER

—3—

Father let out a frustrated snort and thumped his tail against the ground. Garen gave him a sidelong glance and then asked, "So do we go and look for the bandits?"

"I think we should. If we find them, then we will most likely find Mother." I tucked the stone into my satchel, making sure that the handkerchief was tied over it. I had no desire to lose it.

Father began pacing, and his breathing became harsh. His nostrils flared. I could tell that he was angry that someone would do this on purpose. He began to take large gulps of air to calm himself down, and I heard him begin to pray quietly. I prayed silently too. *Oh Lord, help us find Mother before something bad happens to her.*

"Let's go to Appline," Father suggested once his immediate anger subsided.

"Your mother and I were on our way there anyway. If this whole trip was caused by someone from there, just to get us to leave the castle, they're the closest and most reasonable to cause an ambush."

I stopped. I hadn't thought of the possibility of the trip being part of the plot. I turned to Garen.

"Father wants to go to Appline. He thinks someone from there might have been behind the ambush."

"I will follow wherever His Majesty wishes to go. Allow me, Your Highness." He turned and helped boost me up in between Father's shoulders. Then he followed, mounting much easier this time.

Father leaped off the ground and began to beat his wings. As we rose higher and higher, Garen let out his breath anxiously. We flew over the mountains. Garen, still slightly scared, had gotten somewhat used to the motion of flying and was now looking around.

"This is amazing."

I glanced back at him and saw him looking down. "Oh dear …" He paled slightly and looked up at me, "Um … how long is it going to take to get there flying?"

"I don't know," I said with a shrug. What would have taken us three days just to get to the carriage took us just over a couple of hours. Flying was definitely much quicker. I wish I could fly myself.

As Father flew, I continued to pray for Mother and for us. *Lord, please grant us safety and clarity on what to do. Help us to think clearly and … please keep us all safe.*

Just an hour or two later, I saw Appline's castle. Placed with the back half of its kingdom toward the northern mountains, Appline was famous for its trade with the dwellers in the mountains and the northern islands. I marveled at the castle as we flew closer. It was much different than Misby's. Its seven towers were not only taller, they were also slenderer than the ones back home. The blue roofs shone in the afternoon sun like ice. Large windows of clear rock lined its innermost walls.

Father flew over the back courtyard and the double outer wall. With the city in view and the forest just off to the right, I leaned forward to talk to Father.

"Maybe you should land in the forest. That way, you don't scare the people in the city."

Unlike Misby, Appline had very little to no Griffins at all, but they had something that we didn't. They had sort of a problem with rockmals and ice trolls. The ice trolls had often traded things with Appline, but those trading opportunities were very rare. Ice trolls were hard to find and were made of rocks, ice, or snow. They lived up in the northernmost mountains, which were always covered in snow. On the other hand, rockmals—animals formed from just rock—could be found anywhere in the mountains surrounding Appline. Rockmals, whenever they moved, created earthquakes. That was why the windows of the castle were made of clear rock.

We landed in the forest. Father's descent was as silent as the forest itself, except for a flock of birds that we had just disturbed. Garen slipped off Father with much more grace this time and then turned to help me. As I slid off Father's back and into Garen's hands, I heard a noise off to my left. I looked around, and my heart began to pound in my chest. We had landed in a small clearing surrounded by elm trees. Large bushes and other undergrowth covered most of the ground, making it impossible to see if anything was there.

There was a snap of a twig, and Garen quickly pulled me behind him, drawing his sword. Father sniffed the air and frowned. He growled and began to walk to the edge of the clearing. In the next instant, something jumped out from the undergrowth. Father hissed and leaped in front of Garen and me. I flinched as I saw sunlight flash off of five swords. I looked out from around Garen. A band of men, dressed in brown cloaks and with swords drawn, began to circle us. I let out a gasp of fright.

"Stop right—" The leader stopped at my gasp, looking surprised. "Wait … Annabell … is that you?" The man pulled the hood of his cloak off.

I suddenly recognized who this man was.

"Cousin Charles," I said, releasing a sigh of relief.

Father, still eyeing the band of men with a frown, stepped back from in front of Garen and me. Garen had dropped his sword and let out a rush of air.

Cousin Charles was Mother's cousin—the one who was getting married in ten days. Technically, he was my second cousin, but I just called him cousin. He was the same height as Mother and had mousy brown hair that just covered his ears. His sword was drawn, and his men followed suit.

"What are you doing here? And with a Griffin?" he asked, coming closer and giving me a hug. He kept his eyes on Father.

"Well … we have sort of a problem," I said as I pulled myself out of his hug. "Do you know if there are any wizards or magical creatures that we could talk to about this?"

I held up the stone. Father hissed at me, but I ignored him. The guards stiffened at the hiss. Charles looked at it.

"It's just a stone. So why … oh, wait, what does it do?" Garen frowned. I could tell what he was thinking. How could Charles know that it did something without being told?

"Um," I mumbled, glancing at him, "I don't know if I should tell you." I looked over Charles's shoulder at the other guards. He glanced back at them as well.

"Oh, of course. You can tell me at the castle, but …" He trailed off. "I don't think the Griffin should come."

Father growled, "If he thinks for one minute that I'm staying here …"

Charles and his guards suddenly raised their swords defensively against Father. I held up my hands.

"No, don't!" I turned to Charles. "Look, I know that there are no Griffins in this area. Just to let you know for the future, though, this is a gold Griffin. The only ones that you need to worry about are the brown and clay ones. They are not as tame as the golds."

"Oh." Charles's shoulders relaxed, and he and the others returned their swords to their sheaths.

"That's good to know. Well, come. Let's go to the castle." He held out his arm to me. I took it, and we began walking through the trees. Garen and Father followed. I turned to Charles as we came to the edge of the city.

"What were you and your men doing in the woods?"

He shrugged. "We've been having trouble again with the huntsmen from Flying Arrow Woods. They've been on quite a few ambushes recently."

"Oh." I looked at Father. He locked eyes with me. Those bandits could have come from this direction. It was now sunset, and our shadows were long and drawn. The city was much of what I expected for Appline. All houses and buildings were made of stone to protect them from earthquakes. Blue was a common color in building designs, as it was the color of Appline's flag. As we walked through the streets, people stopped and stared. Father let out a snort, and a child nearby took cover behind his mother's skirts.

Garen, who was getting wistful glances from a few girls, quickened his pace. He was feeling uncomfortable. We reached the castle not long after, and Garen and Father let out a sigh of relief. The palace guards opened the doors to the grand hall, and we walked inside. As I stepped through the door, I stopped and dropped my arm from Charles's grip.

When we arrived at the castle, I expected it to be fully decorated for Charles's wedding, to which my parents had been invited. There was nothing. No banners. No garlands. No flowers. Just the grand hall with all its normal tapestries.

"Well," Father said, coming in behind me and sitting down, "This is not what I expected for a person who is getting married in ten days."

The guards quickly closed the main doors at Father's noise. I nodded, confused.

"I agree," I said out loud, forgetting that no one else could understand him.

"To what?" Charles asked, turning around. He was well into the grand hall, so his voice echoed.

"Why aren't there any decorations?" I asked, a little embarrassed.

"Decorations?" Charles repeated, confused.

I felt myself blush. "For your wedding," I mumbled.

Charles burst into laughter that echoed loudly around the room. "My wedding! Ha! Oh, Annabell, where did you hear that?"

The heat in my cheeks subsided, and now it was my turn to stare, confused.

"Didn't you send Mother and Father an invitation?"

Charles shook his head. "I did not. I am not planning on getting married anytime soon."

Father let out a low growl, and Garen folded his arms.

Charles ignored them. "Now regarding what you have " … He paused and glanced at the guards by the doors. "Come with me. Your Griffin and guard might want to stay here." He turned and continued walking.

I followed and then turned and looked at Father and Garen. Their expressions matched mine. Confused. Charles led me out of the grand hall and up a flight of stairs. He called out to a passing maid, "See to it that rooms are prepared for Princess Annabell and her guard."

The maid curtsied and hurried down the stairs. When she was gone, Charles continued, "The best way to answer your question is in my study." He rounded a corner. "Here we are." He pulled a key out of his pocket and unlocked the big wooden door. He held it open and ushered me inside.

I stared in amazement. There were shelves all around the room. There was not one bit of wall space that didn't have a shelf or something on the shelf covering it. The only light in the room was let in by a large window on one wall. I gazed at the shelves. Each one of them held some colored liquid, books, and other objects. I stopped at a shelf. There was a bottle of glowing light.

"May I have the stone?" Charles asked as he came in and sat down at a worktable in the center of the room. It was covered with paper and books. I tore my gaze from the bottle and opened my satchel and handed him the stone wrapped in a handkerchief.

"So where did you find it?" Charles asked as he carefully opened the tied cloth and set the stone on his worktable. I glanced around the room again. Charles was an apritorius wizard, meaning that he wasn't completely a wizard, but he knew some magic. The shelves that lined the walls of the study made the large room feel crowded.

"By my father's carriage."

"What does it do?" He reached for a book that was leaning on the edge of the table but kept his eyes on the stone.

"It—I don't think I should tell you. But can you find out who made it?" He looked at me as he reached for another book.

"Unfortunately, I can only find out if anyone in this kingdom made it. My magical knowledge does not allow me to go beyond that."

He brought the book down from the shelf and flipped a couple of pages.

"Here we are. Just a minute, and I'll be able to tell you." Placing his fingertips on the edge of the handkerchief, he muttered something, and there was a quick burst of light that fell on the stone. When it faded, he shook his head, tied the handkerchief closed, and handed it back to me.

"Sorry, no one here made it."

I sighed and put the stone back in my satchel. "Thank you anyway, Charles." I glanced out the window. The sun was gone, but the light in the sky reflected into the room.

"It's too late to leave now. Do you mind if we leave tomorrow?"

"You're quite welcome. It's not often that I get to do that sort of thing. Your rooms should be ready by now."

He led me out the door. I thanked him again and went back to the grand hall. Father and Garen were still there, looking tired and thoroughly bored. Garen brightened when he saw me.

"So? Did you find out anything?" I shook my head, and his shoulders slumped

"Only that it wasn't made here. I think we should all pray."

Garen nodded, and Father lay down so that his head was level with ours. I began to pray out loud.

"Lord, you know that what we are going through is very difficult. Help us to just trust and honor you through it all. I pray that you would give us strength and patience to go on. Help us to know which way to go and direct our path. I also pray for Mother that you will keep her safe and that we can find her quickly." I paused. "Your will be done, Lord."

Garen picked up my prayer. "Lord and God, I pray for those who attacked and captured Queen Casia. I pray that through some way, you will help them to come to you and to realize what they did was wrong. Give King Harold and Princess Annabell peace and comfort through this time. Thank you for your help in the past times Lord. Amen."

"Amen," both Father and I echoed.

Father stood and stretched and then let out a roaring yawn that startled both me and Garen. It echoed around the large grand hall, sounding louder than it actually was. The maid I had seen on the way to Charles's study was coming into the hall. She jumped at the noise. At the sight of her, I turned to Garen.

"Charles had rooms made for us so we can stay the night and then continue looking tomorrow."

"Wonderful," Garen muttered, yawning as well. The maid motioned for us to follow her. She was frightened by Father; her eyes were wide. As I came up to her side, I said, "You don't need to be afraid."

I went on to explain about Griffins, and she seemed to relax slightly.

"I don't think there would be a bedroom big enough to fit him," she said quietly.

Father heard her anyway. "I'd rather have more room anyway." Father ended up staying in the grand hall. He ruffled his feathers and lay down. The maid flinched at the squawking she heard and then let out a relieved sigh as he lay down. She led Garen and me to our rooms. They were just off of the grand hall. Garen's room was across from mine.

"Good night, Your Highness," Garen said, bowing as he went into his room. As I opened the door to mine, I was suddenly overcome by sleep. I hadn't realized how tired I was till now. I didn't bother getting undressed. I was too tired. I took my shoes off and let out a sigh. I fell back onto the bed. As soon as my head touched the pillow, I fell asleep.

When I woke up again it was still night, and as the wind blew in through the window, the sound of chimes came with it. Chimes? Where was that coming from? I rolled over onto my side and began thinking about what had happened today. None of it made any sense. If no wizard had made it here … then who? It could literally be anyone. My thoughts wandered to Charles's supposed wedding. I rolled onto my back, the sound of chimes still ringing in my ears.

The wedding confused me the most. Before I had said good night to him, I had asked Father if the invitation he and Mother received was a letter or words from a messenger. He had told me that it had been a letter. I stared up at the ceiling. Who would have taken the time to create an official-looking invitation?

My original thought was that if it had been a messenger that was sent, someone could have sent them to get Mother and Father to leave. But when he said it had been a letter … I didn't know what to think. My mind kept circulating the question, *Who?* The rest of the night I spent half sleep, half awake, thinking with the chimes keeping me up.

I woke to the streams of light filling the sky. I rubbed my eyes, trying to get them to adjust. It was dawn. Quickly I changed into a new dress, realizing that the one I had worn to bed last night was now a wrinkled mess. After brushing my hair and braiding it again,

I grabbed my things and rushed out of the room into the grand hall. Garen was already there, eating what he had taken from the dining hall. Charles was with him and had a sack in his hands. Father sat beside him looking like he hadn't slept at all. Charles turned as I came into the hall.

"Ah, there you are, Annabell. Here, I prepared a sack of food for a couple of days." He handed the provisions to me.

"Thank you. Thank you again for letting us stay the night."

He nodded. Garen finished a biscuit he had been eating.

"Are you ready to go, Your Highness?" He wiped his hands on his pants.

I nodded, grabbing my own biscuit out of the sack. After saying goodbye to Charles, we walked out into the courtyard. I flung my two satchels across my shoulder, and Garen gave me a boost up onto Father's back. Garen swung himself up after me. He was getting better at mounting and dismounting. Once we were seated, Father leaped off into the sky. I looked at Father and Garen. They both looked tired. Garen had dark circles around his eyes, and Father's eyelids drooped. I shook my head trying to shake off the tiredness I felt. None of us had gotten much sleep last night.

"Where ... should we ... go now?" I asked as loudly as I could. It was hard to talk when the wind was filling your mouth.

"Let's try Fizenburg. I know someone there that could give us some information," Garen said, managing to avoid catching a draft of air in his mouth. I glanced back at him. He seemed to enjoy flying now.

Father didn't say anything, but he turned in the direction of Fizenburg. If one could fly, like we were doing now, they would have to go over the ocean to get to Fizenburg because in between Appline and Fizenburg was a huge forest. It was dubbed Flying Arrow Woods, and for a good reason. The woodsmen and bandits who lived there were often known for shooting down anything that flew overhead, and they never missed. Pets and wild animals had suffered the consequences. I only knew this because one of our guards had gone hunting near the woods with his hawk. It never came back, so he had gone into the woods to find it and met up with a woodsman holding his hawk after shooting it.

In addition to their accuracy, the woodsmen and their families were never friendly, and they trusted no one. None of the three kingdoms wanted to claim the forest, so the woodsmen ruled themselves. I glanced back at the forest as we started flying over the ocean. It was dark and menacing with its tall trees. I shuddered to think what could have happened if we had flown over. I faced forward again. There were miles of open ocean, and off to Father's right was an island. The wind whistled past my ears.

Everything around us seemed silent. Garen leaned forward so he could be heard. "Is it just me, or does something feel wrong?"

I glanced over at him and listened. There was nothing. Because we were flying over the ocean, a cool draft of air was coming up from underneath us. The air felt hollow and empty as it rushed past us. I shivered and nodded. As we traveled on, the wrongness of the air began to make me more and more uncomfortable.

I leaned close to Father's ear. "Can we land real quick? Something doesn't feel right." He nodded and started to spiral downward. The island was below us, and its closest point formed into a cliff. Father landed on a cliff of the island. It was the only spot that I had seen that wasn't covered in oak and elm trees. Father crouched, and I slid off his back along with Garen.

"Did you feel it too?" Father asked, standing up again. He glanced around at the cliff and the trees quickly, looking worried.

"Yes, I did," I said, slightly shaking. I looked around, not quite sure what was causing the wrong feeling. The air was still, and it seemed to echo the slightest sound. The hair on the back of my neck stood. Someone was there watching us. I listened and looked carefully around. The cliff we had landed on was just on the outer edge of the thick forest ahead of us. A wind picked up and blew through the trees toward us, bringing the sound of small gongs.

Garen's eyes widened, and Father's head shot up. His feathered ears came straight up.

Garen looked around rapidly. "What was that?"

I drew in a breath and stared into the woods where the sound came from. I had read about that sound in my tutoring, but I had never actually heard it.

"Fairies."

Father hissed, and Garen quickly drew his sword. Fairies were known to be mischievous. The only thing was that they were considered legends and were said to have lived on an island. Most people had said, or at least thought, that the fairies were mischievous, but not cruel. No one had ever found the island or had encountered a fairy. I looked around again. I didn't think the island would be this close to land. I turned that thought over in my mind.

I looked toward Father. "We have to go in."

"Wait, what? Are you sure? Why?" Garen asked, lowering his sword just the tiniest bit.

I nodded. "Because they might have something to do with the stone. The island is not that far from the continent, and they have magic. They could have easily created the stone and then sent it to the bandits in the woods."

"Why would they want to change your mother and me, though? I have never had an encounter with a fairy," Father said, cocking his head.

I shrugged.

"I don't know. The best way to find out would be to ask them. Right?" I turned toward the woods and started forward. The wind blew through the trees again, but this time bringing the sound of chimes. I paused. Chimes again? That wasn't a fairy sound. I felt a slight tug on my satchel.

"Um … Your Highness?" Garen said, sounding worried.

"What?" I turned, thinking it was him holding the satchel. I gasped. My satchel had come off my shoulder and was floating just a few feet away from me. I stared at it as it slowly sank to the ground. All three of us looked at it wide eyed.

Garen, standing maybe two steps away, carefully tapped it with the tip of his sword. The satchel didn't move again. I let out a sigh of relief. When nothing happened, I walked back to it. I knelt down and carefully opened the top. Nothing looked out of place. I carefully started looking through and realized that something was out of place. I looked in, and my eyes widened. Garen and Father came closer.

"Oh no, oh no" I muttered, beginning to search frantically.

"What? Annabell, what's the matter?" Father said, coming up over my shoulder and looking into the satchel. I looked up at him, even more worried.

"The stone is gone."

CHAPTER

—4—

I stared blankly into my satchel. How had I lost it? I check the corners of the satchel to see if it has slipped there. The handkerchief that I used to hold it wasn't there anymore. All of it was gone. I sat back trying to think. Charles had given it back to me, and I had put it in my satchel. So where was it? I had never let it get too far out of my reach, and I had purposely tied the handkerchief closed so it could not fall out. Garen stared at me wide eyed, along with Father.

"You lost it?!" Father yelled.

"Are you sure it's not in there?" Garen said, coming to look into the bag himself.

"Yes!" I said, showing him the bag. "I don't know where it … wait a minute." I stood up, closed my satchel, and put it back on. "Did either of you hear chimes just now?"

Garen stood up, and both of them nodded their heads.

"And then my satchel started floating," I said, holding out my hands to see if they were catching what I was trying to say.

Garen's eyes suddenly lit up, beginning to see what I meant.

"So that means—" Garen started, and I cut him off.

"That magic was used. Again." I looked at Father and then glanced at the woods behind me.

"Don't tell me you think it was the fairies," Father said, following my gaze. He looked rather irritated about the whole matter and was not pleased that the stone had disappeared.

"I'm afraid I do. Now we have to go see them." I turned to go into the woods.

"Begging your pardon for asking, but what did His Majesty say?" Garen asked, glancing at Father.

"Oh, I'm sorry," I said, glancing at him. "I keep forgetting that you can't understand him. He asked me if I thought it was the fairies' magic."

I heard Garen let out a small groan but ignored it. I started walking into the trees. Garen and Father would follow. At least, I was pretty sure they would. I looked over my shoulder at them when I had gotten a few paces under the branches. Father let out a sigh and started forward. Garen resheathed his sword. I continued forward now with a smile. I felt more confident.

"I don't like this at all," Garen said as he whacked away a low tree branch with his sword. He had taken it out again when the foliage got thicker. He was in front of me now, whacking at another tree branch. Leaves began to fall, and I quickly put my cloak's hood up to protect my hair.

"What if they're around us right now?" he said, continuing the path forward.

I nodded. "They could attack, and we wouldn't even know it."

The sound of the gongs seemed to come from everywhere. The forest was dark, and only small shafts of lights came through the trees. One second, the forest would seem wide open to the canopy above our heads. The next, it seemed almost too thick to pass through. The strangest thing, though, was that there were no sounds other than the gongs. No birds. No small animals. Nothing.

I turned to Father, who was snarling at a branch that he had just run into. I held back a laugh.

"Do you suppose—" I started but was cut off abruptly when the gongs became so loud that I had to cover my ears with my hands. The wind picked up, blowing leaves and twigs everywhere. It whipped my hood off my head and threw my cloak around. Garen nearly fell over. His sword was blown from his hand. It fell only a few feet away, but the wind was too strong for him to pick it up. Father yelled in surprise and leaned into the wind. It began pushing him, and I nearly fell over myself. Then suddenly, Father was gone. The sound of the gongs stopped, but the wind kept up, still pushing everything it could. I lowered my hands from my ears and tried to pull my hair out of my face. My eyes flowed over everything, trying to find Father.

Garen, who had crouched to the ground, looked around wildly and yelled above the wind, "Where did he go?"

I was about to reply when the sound of the gongs grew loud again, along with the wind. My hands went up to my ears again. With my hands protecting my ears, I couldn't grab on to anything. The wind pushed me back against the trunk of a tree. The wind had gotten so loud and strong that I couldn't hear anything and had to keep my eyes closed. Terrified, I prayed, "Lord! Help us! Please help us!"

The strength of the wind lessened, and I turned to look for Garen, but he was gone.

"Garen?" I yelled as loud as I could. "GAREN?" The wind died, and everything became still again. I removed my hands from my ears. It was silent. I looked quickly around, concerned that someone was watching me. I picked up Garen's sword, thinking that I would give it back to him if I found him. Then I heard a quiet giggle and the gongs began to echo again. Laughter followed the giggle, replacing the sound of the gongs.

I stepped out from the tree that I had been pushed against and turned in a circle, trying to pinpoint where the laughter was coming from. "All right, I know that you fairies live here. Come out! Now!" I yelled.

One of the fairies (or at least that's what I thought it was) stopped laughing. The others continued their tittering as the one spoke. "Ha. She can't even understand what we are saying. She doesn't even know that we're right around her."

The fairy started laughing with the others again. I had guessed right. They were fairies. Creatures. That was why I could understand them when any other person would hear gongs. I felt my face grow hot as I grew angry. Inwardly, I prayed for strength and the right words to say.

"Well, I do know that you're there. I can understand you, fairies, you know. Come out now!" I yelled again and walked up to where I had heard the fairy speak.

Their laughter stopped, and a breeze gently stirred through the air. Leaves and twigs were brought into tight circles in five different spots around me, and the fairies appeared. The leaves and twigs settled on the ground again.

"You can ... understand us?" asked the fairy I was standing in front of.

I stared at her for a moment and looked around at the others. The fairies were not what I had pictured them to be. They were all the size of adults. The fairy that had spoken to me had black hair and green eyes. Her pale skin made the features on her face stand out more. Her dress was made of ... well, what looked like a tornado. The fairy's skin faded as it met a gray clouded whirlwind that swirled into the form of a dress. All the others around me had the same apparel as well. None of the fairies had wings. They just hovered over the ground. I refocused my attention on her.

"Yes, I can. Now please return my friends," I said, placing my hand on my hip while the other still grasped the sword. The corner of her mouth slowly lifted into a smirk. She seemed rather arrogant, and it made me the slightest bit annoyed. The fairy glanced at the others and then looked at me, and the quiet chuckling started again.

42

"Why?"

"Excuse me?" I was a little surprised at her question. Laughter followed my question.

"Why do you need them?"

I stared at her. She was purposely making things difficult. I could hear it in her voice. I silently prayed for strength again and responded.

"The same reason you need yours. For company …support… friendship."

"Why—wait, what?" The fairy was taken aback. She had been prepared to go on with the why question again and was stunned at my response. The other fairies had stopped their laughter too at my response.

I repeated myself, "The same reason you need your friends. For company, support, and friendship."

She stared at me. Then she began slowly, "That … that's a good answer. Right?" She turned to the others. They all stared at me silently but nodded. I sighed when nothing was said for a few moments.

"Look, I just want my friends back. Can you bring them back? Or can you show me where they are so I can get them?"

The fairies continued to stare. Finally, the one I had been speaking to nodded. "Come with me."

"Thank you," I said and followed her.

As she led me through the foliage, the other fairies stood there whispering to each other. What was the matter with them? I turned my attention back to my guide. We went deeper and deeper into the forest. Less and less light shone through the trees. Branches and bushes grew closer together, making it nearly impossible for me to see where I was placing my foot, not to mention I also had to carry the sword with me. The fairy remained silent. She easily made her way through the plants, but she did not seem thoroughly pleased with something. Was it me? Had I said something back at the tree that was wrong? As I stepped over a moss-covered log, I suddenly

heard more voices. They were not altogether clear, as we were still quite far away from them.

"What is it? We know … but what is … this?" said the first speaker I heard. The voice sounded like it belonged to some younger woman.

"Well, it's not a Drafgon, or a lefren … I'm not sure," a second voice replied. This woman sounded rather tired with the discussion that had taken place before I heard them. The second voice seemed to try to end the conversation with the sentence she had just spoken. A third voice quickly followed. This woman sounded frustrated.

"Well … of course not, silly! It has feathers and fur! It has to be …"

I stepped under another branch. *Oh, they're talking about Father.* It had never occurred to me that fairies did not know what a Griffin was. The arguing continued as the fairy led me into a sun-filled clearing. I blinked at the sudden light. With one step, all the trees and bushes disappeared. I looked around. The clearing was beautiful. There were flowers everywhere that shone like gems. They grew on the ground, on bushes, and even on the trunks of some of the trees facing the clearing. The flowers only grew facing the light; none of them were growing in the forest. Balls of light, like the one I had seen in Charles's study, were nestled together with leaves and other plants in strands woven throughout the elm trees. Though the sun was directly overhead, the globes of light still let off a soft glow into the clearing.

The three voices I had heard arguing were three fairies standing off to one side of the clearing. They were still debating with each other and hadn't noticed that the fairy and I were there. I looked around the clearing, trying to find Father and Garen. I looked over at the three fairies again. They were standing over by a tree, whose roots had been raised from beneath the ground. I stared wide eyed at the roots. Father was beneath them, pacing angrily. He locked eyes with me as he walked to one side of the roots and yelled, "Annabell!"

45

The three fairies, startled by his roar, instantly stopped arguing and faced him.

"Father!" I called out, running to him. The youngest-looking one whipped her head around and stared at me. She was dressed in rose-petal pink. The dress she wore reached the ground and was folded in such a way to look like rose petals. There were no sleeves, just two straps that were parallel to the top of her shoulders. Her hazel eyes were a contrast to her blond hair, which fell just between her shoulder blades. Around her ponytail was a garland of flowers. As I ran past the three of them, I saw that she seemed shocked that I was there. She looked at the fairy who had brought me here. Father tried to break the roots as I came closer. I set Garen's sword down next to me and began to help him. I heard the fairies begin to talk again.

"Ventus, you're back. Why ... or how come she's with you?" I glanced back at the fairies. They didn't seem the least bit concerned that I was trying to help Father escape.

"She ended it, Omnia. I didn't even get to the second 'why.'" Ventus, the fairy who had led me through the woods, shrugged. Omnia, the one in pink, stared at her wide-eyed. I momentarily paused at the root I had been pulling. Ventus had been playing a game with me? I frowned and continued pulling, looking at them over my shoulder.

"She did?!" the second fairy said, surprised. She was wearing a green dress. Long layers of fabric made it look flowy. It had a single short sleeve on her left shoulder, and it too was loose. She had a wreath of leaves woven into her golden brown hair on the top of her head. Her eyes were blue, and they gave her face a pleasant look. Ventus exhaled in a way that sounded irritated.

"Yes, she did, Ligna. Now, can you—"

"Not yet." The third fairy placed her hands on her hips. Her hair was a rusty amber color and reached the middle of her back with two long strands of hair that rested against her shoulders. She was wearing a brown shirt with no sleeves, and the bottom of it covered the top of her brown skirt. Her light-brown eyes flashed with annoyance.

"She has to tell us what that is. And also why she called it, Father. Where she's from—"

"Silvestris, do we have to do this every time someone comes here?" Omnia asked, rolling her eyes. I turned from the fairies as they started arguing again and looked back at the roots. Father was having no success tearing the roots. He let out an angry sigh and sat down. My hands slipped from the root I was pulling, and I nearly fell backward. I looked at him and rubbed my palm.

"Are you all right?" I whispered. "Where's Garen?"

"I'm right here." Garen walked around from the other side of the tree.

I glanced behind him, and he shook his head.

"No luck. I couldn't even dig into the ground." I picked up his sword and handed it to him through the roots.

"Here is your sword. Do you think you could dig a hole with that?"

He put it back in its sheath. "I doubt it. His Majesty couldn't claw through the roots or the ground."

"Other than not being able to get out of here, we're fine," Father said with a huff. He looked rather frazzled and was very irritated. Garen walked up to the roots and looked behind me, and I turned and followed his gaze. The fairies were still arguing.

"I wonder why they did this. Excuse me?" Garen called out.

I turned to Father again.

"Are you sure that you are okay?"

He nodded. The fairies' talking subsided at Garen's call, and I heard Omnia whisper.

"Look! She's talking to it!" I tried staying focused on Father. I knew that they would start talking to me if I looked their way.

"Did you find the pebble? Did you have time to look or ask for it?" I asked quickly.

"No," he said with a rush of air.

"That wind fairy is coming over." Garen took a step back from the roots. I let out a sigh. I didn't feel like talking to them. Again I prayed for strength and the ability to give the fairies grace. I glanced back at them. Ventus raised her hand. It caused a whirlwind to come my way and turn me around. I shuddered. It felt strange being turned and not actually controlling the movement. I looked at her. She was only a few paces away from the other fairies.

"Yes?"

"Can you come talk with us?" she said quietly, looking over at me. She was eyeing Father and didn't look particularly comfortable with him.

I looked at Father, then at her, and nodded. I came back with her to the other side, and Omnia asked, "So … what is that … exactly?" she said, pointing to Father, who was grumbling and muttering something inaudible. "It's not your pet, is it?"

I shook my head.

"I told you!" Silvestris burst out, folding her arms and giving Omnia a triumphant grin. Ligna rolled her eyes.

"No, it's not my pet."

I heard Father let out a loud snort at the idea, and I continued, "He's a gold Griffin. They won't hurt you. They're the tamest ones that exist." I told them the rest about Griffins and what they should know.

"But why did you call it Father?" Ligna asked, giving me a confused look.

"Because …" I trailed off. What should I tell them? As I was thinking, I heard Father yell, and I glanced at him.

"Ask them about the stone first! Whatever they just said, don't answer till you've asked them first!" he hissed, passing his side of the cage.

I turned, remembering, at Father's statement, that he and Garen couldn't understand the fairies. Facing Ventus, I prayed for confidence as I was very nervous to ask her about the stone. I hoped that she wouldn't get angry. I quickly let out a rush of air and said to Ventus, "Where's the stone?"

The four of them stared at me, confused. "What stone?" Omnia asked. Her eyes were puzzled.

"You're trying to change the subject!" Silvestris snapped. Her hands flew upward in frustration.

"I'm not telling you any more until you give me it," I replied, folding my arms.

Ventus and Ligna looked at each other and then at me and said at the same time, "What stone are you talking about?"

I blinked and turned to them.

"Wait, you don't have it?"

They shook their heads, and again, Ventus asked, "What stone?"

I was nearly too shocked to speak. Garen called out from the cage, "What did she say?"

When I repeated my own questions and Ventus's reply, Father roared in frustration. Ligna jumped at the sound and her hands went flying up in the air. A spell flew from her fingers and hit Father and Garen's cage. The roots opened just for a split second, but it was enough time for Father to tear out of the cage. Sprinting as fast as he could go, he sped across the clearing. I jumped back and yelled in fright as he came running by and jumped on top of Ventus.

CHAPTER

—5—

"Father!" I yelled, forgetting momentarily that the fairies were standing there. "Get off of her!"

"Who did you give it to?" he hissed.

He had knocked her over and had pinned her to the ground. It was a very strange scene, since half of her was just a gray whirlwind. He was leaning over her with his face less than an inch away from hers. The others had gone frantic trying to use spells to get him off of her. I was praying that none of them would do any damage to him. Light flashed from their fingers, but it soon dissipated when they reached Father. I thanked God for answering my prayer.

"Get off of me!" Ventus said angrily, but her eyes were filled with terror. She grabbed the forearm of Father's front right paw and tried to lift it from her shoulder. I ran up to Father's ear on the same side.

"She can't understand you any more than you can understand her, remember? Now, please, get off of her," I whispered.

"Tell her what I said first," Father said with a growl.

I turned to Ventus, who had given up on trying to lift the paw that held her down. She lay there quietly fuming.

"We never had it," Ligna answered, trying to create a plant that would pull Father away. It withered within an inch of Father's flank.

Omnia and Silvestris nodded when I looked at them. They had stopped their frantic hand waving and stared at Father, confused that their spells weren't working. I told Father their reply, and he reluctantly let Ventus up. She scowled at him as she got up and went to stand next to Silvestris, who was the farthest away from Father.

I stared at them again "You didn't have it? Then where ..." I trailed off, trying to think where it could have gone.

"Um ... I don't mean to interrupt anything, Your Highness—"

"Your Highness?" Silvestris whispered to Ventus.

I turned. Garen had not been able to get out of the cage as quickly as Father and was caught halfway in between. It looked rather uncomfortable.

Garen continued, "Could you possibly ask them to let me go?"

"Oh! Sorry, Garen!" I said, giving him a concerned look. I faced Ventus, Silvestris, Omnia, and Ligna.

"Could one of you release him please?"

Oh! Sure. I almost forgot he was there," Ligna said. She rotated her hand, and the roots of the tree disappeared.

"Thank you both," Garen said, walking toward our group while rolling his shoulder.

"You're quite welcome," I said with a smile. Ligna just gave him a slight nod. Silvestris came up to Garen's side, and his hand jumped to the hilt of his sword.

"No! It's okay, Garen. She isn't going to do anything to you," I said, quickly grabbing the sword's hilt myself. He relaxed, his hand dropping to his side.

"What do you mean by calling her 'Your Highness'?" Silvestris asked Garen.

He stared at her blankly and then turned to me for clarification.

"What did she say?" I ignored his question and turned to respond to Silvestris myself. "He can't understand you. Only I can because I was born with the ability to talk to things that are alive and that aren't …"—I paused, trying to think of how to put it—"human."

I shook my head at the thought and continued, "He said 'Your Highness' because I am a princess. Princess Annabelle of Misby."

"Oh my!" Ligna gasped, and she covered her mouth with her hand. Ventus grew pale and, momentarily, stood looking at the ground wide eyed.

"We are so sorry for the way we treated you and your friends, Your Highness," Omnia said, going into a deep curtsy and nearly falling over.

The others followed and nearly fell over themselves.

"Oh … no, it's fine. I understand that you didn't know," I said, pulling her off the ground.

The four of them stood. Silvestris gave Father a suspicious look but then turned to me with a smile.

"We would be honored if you and your company would stay the night. Just as long as the Griffin doesn't jump on anyone."

Father hissed, and she jumped.

I put my hand up to stop him from doing anything else. "He won't."

At this, Father let out an irritated snort, which meant I would have to explain my thinking later. Lowering my arm, I said to the fairies, "We would love to stay the night."

Father sat next to Garen, who was off to my right, mumbling unhappily.

Hours later, the sun had set, and the clearing was now full of activity. The globes of light floated in the trees and lit the clearing. Ventus, Silvestris, Omnia, and Ligna set up a banquet in our honor. Fairies of all sizes and colors had come into the clearing. Ventus had sent them messages through the wind that a princess was here with her friends and that help preparing a banquet was needed. Now hundreds of fairies flew about hanging flowers and setting up fires. The four fairies flew about calling out instructions and setting a table near the outer edge of the clearing.

"So why are we still here?" Father asked, looking around unhappily. We were on the edge of the clearing observing the activity. I gently rested my hand on his shoulder, which was near my head.

"I wanted to stay because we could ask them who made it. I am sure that they have some ability to test that." Garen sat down on a fallen log.

"I just hope that they will answer your questions, Your Highness."

I thought for a moment. "Well, I can try asking now. Excuse me"—I gently tapped the arm of a fairy that came by—"could you ask Silvestris to come over?"

The fairy, who was dressed in deep red with blond hair, smiled.

"Of course, Your Highness." Minutes later, Silvestris came over, seeming happy to help.

"Yes?"

"I was wondering, is there any way possible for you to find out where the stone is and who made it?"

She scrunched up her face, trying to think. "One moment, let me try." She turned her hand, palm up, and thrust her fingers up into the air as though she was holding something. A soft glow of light appeared and then danced in the air above her hand, leaving a sparkling trail. It grew bright for a second, but then fizzled out. Her hand relaxed, and her face dropped in disappointment.

"I'm sorry. I think it's too far away for me to find it." She gave me a sympathetic look and gently clasped her hands in front of her, "If you had it with you, Your Highness, I would have been able to tell you who made it, but without it here …" She trailed off.

My shoulders dropped slightly in dismay. First, we lost Mother, and now the stone. Things were getting so complicated.

"Oh, well ... thank you for at least trying." Silvestris gave a brief nod and then flew off to continue with preparations.

I sighed and sat down next to Garen.

"They can't find it with their magic, can they?" he asked.

I shook my head, "Nope, they can't. I don't know what to do." I leaned my head against Father's side.

"Well," Father said slowly, "I have one option." I looked up at him, and he gave me a half smile. "Pray." I gave him a tired smile in return.

"Of course. Let's do that now." Garen came over and sat to my right. Seated in a circle, the three of us prayed for hope, peace, and the strength to endure. We also prayed that whoever had the stone would soon be shown to us. The time between then to the banquet was spent in prayer.

We were flying again the next day. The night with the fairies had been somewhat chaotic. Although it had been enjoyable to see them dance, I was glad we were leaving. They were too loud, and often got into arguments. Father's anger about staying the night with them and being kept in a cage had subsided and given way to forgiveness.

"They didn't know who I was," he had said as we took to the air. He was, however, very disturbed that the stone was still missing.

"Do you realize that if that ... *thing* got into the wrong hands ... what might happen?" He said as we flew over the rolling hills north of Fizenburg.

Look what already has happened, I thought, gently patting Father's back. I looked at the landscape below us, thinking. We had gone nearly everywhere on the continent, and there was still no sign of Mother, her captors, or the stone. When we had left the island, it had been decided that Fizenburg was the last place that needed to be searched. We all unanimously felt that it was what

God wanted us to do. I reflected on how much time we had already spent looking. It had been only three days since we started, but it had seemed much longer. I turned from my thoughts and focused on the landscape.

Below us, in between two hills, was a river. Its water was clear, and even from up in the sky, you could see all the way to the bottom. I looked at the sky. It had taken all morning to cross the ocean from the island, and it took another four hours to fly around the end of the woods. We had been traveling all day, and the sun was now setting. Father had descended to the rolling hills only once for rest, and that had been an hour ago.

I looked at the map that I had in my satchel. Fizenburg was not much farther, but I felt like stopping for the night. It was the last of the three kingdoms on the Northern Continent. It was also much different than the other two. As opposed to being surrounded by mountains, Fizenburg was on a large island, along with a few of its cities, in the middle of an even bigger lake. Most of the kingdom consisted of the rolling hills we were now flying over. I gazed at the sky. The sun had dipped below the horizon, making it darker and impossible to read the map. I glanced down. I could no longer see the ground, but the river caught the last bit of light in the sky.

As I put the map away, Garen tapped me on the shoulder. "Your Highness? It's getting dark," he said, echoing my thoughts. "We should probably stop for the night."

I nodded and leaned forward toward Father's ear. "Can you land?"

He nodded and was starting a downward spiral toward the river when suddenly something exploded below us. Streaks of light shot up into the sky, blocking our view from the ground. BOOM! I screamed as the thunderous sound shook the air around us and nearly caused me to fall off of Father's back. Garen leaned forward, keeping me from falling, and yelled to be heard over the noise. "Your Majesty! Please land!"

"I'm trying!" Father yelled back.

The streams of light continuously shot up into the air. Extreme heat followed the light. Whoever was firing was trying to hit us out of the sky. There was a pause in the streaks, and Father landed just on the other side of one of the two hills.

Garen leaped off Father with his sword drawn just as the streaks started again. They were no longer aimed up at the sky but toward us. Explosions followed each streak, shaking the ground and the air.

I slid off Father's back as one came flying over my head. I ducked behind Garen, out of fear. My heart was beating in my ears. The darkness of the night had covered us. We should have been hidden from whoever was firing. The night was no help. No matter which way we ran, the streaks of light followed. What was even more upsetting was that we could not see who was firing. They were hidden by all the light that shot toward us.

Father was off to my left and had tucked his wings close to his body. He stopped moving and began to dodge the light as it came by. Garen followed Father's lead and began to wield his sword against the streaks of light. He started slashing at them, and each time they hit his sword, they sent sparks flying. I crouched to the ground as he hit one. It dimmed and flew up into the sky. I stared wide eyed at it as it fell to the ground, a foot away from my hand.

"Garen!" I yelled. "They're rocks!"

"What?"

He slashed at another. "They're rocks! Whoever made these must have also made the stone!" Garen swung his sword and looked at me. "Pray that I don't weaken quickly. It could hit you if I do." He brought his sword down on another rock. It split in half.

I began fervently praying, and I heard Father join in as well. The rocks kept flying, and suddenly their light dimmed slightly. The moon had risen and lit up the night.

Garen pointed ahead as his sword caused another stone to go flying, "Look!"

I squinted into the darkness. The moon lit up a large group of men coming over the nearest hill with machines that were firing the lit-up rocks. The streaks of light came with more force, and the sound nearly became deafening.

Garen's sword was nearly thrust out of his hands by a stone as he yelled, "It's the Fizenburg army. They're the ones firing!"

"Why are they attacking us? And why out here?"

Garen said nothing. He was too busy protecting me and himself. Hours passed, and the flight of rocks didn't seem to have an end. Garen's slashing slowed as he grew tired and Father was getting hit more. He would hiss as it hit and left singed feathers in its wake. I prayed the entire time. I had no other option but *to* pray.

"Lord! Help us! Please keep us safe!" I prayed those words over and over again.

Silence filled the night, save the noise of the firing. Suddenly a rock shot through Garen's legs, and I jumped to the right, out from behind him. In the next instant, there was an explosion. A very large explosion. A very, *very* large explosion. An enormous rock shot toward me. The explosion caused a visible ripple in the air that followed it. I screamed as pain tore through my body. Then darkness.

CHAPTER

— 6 —

A brightness filled my eyes as I opened them. I had fallen on my back and was now staring up at the sky. It was early morning, and it was quiet. No wind. No explosions. Not even the Fizenburg army could be heard. Where had they gone? I sat up and moaned as my movement made my legs sore. Sitting there and gently rubbing them, I looked to my left where Garen should have been. I screamed and quickly stood up. Garen was flat on his back, his sword an inch from his fingers. His face was pale, and his eyes were staring straight upward. He was dead.

"No! Lord, please, no!" I cried, covering my face with my hands. I turned away from him and saw Father.

"No! NO!" I yelled and ran over to him, stumbling and crying along the way.

Father lay on his side with his wings open behind him. His blue eyes stared straight ahead. He had died too.

"Please ... Please, Lord! Please, no." I fell in a heap at Father's side. My body trembled in sorrow. As tears rolled down my cheeks, they fell and puddled on the ground. My crying eased up. I rested my hand on his head. It was cold and lifeless. His golden fur was disheveled, and most of it was now black from burns. More sobs shook my body, and my tears fell onto his face.

"Please bring him back, Lord … I … I don't know what to do without him," I cried again, unable to pray aloud more. I put my face in my hands and sat there with tears flowing down my face.

"Your Highness?"

I turned, abruptly stopping my crying so whoever was calling me wouldn't see that I had been. No one was around me. I stood and frantically looked around the rolling green hills

"Your Highness?" It came again, and I couldn't find which direction the voice was coming from. It seemed to come from everywhere and above me. I looked up … and I opened my eyes and found myself staring straight into Garen's face. I felt his arm behind my neck and the other one under my knees. He was carrying me. We were no longer in the hills, and no one was dead. I took a quick breath of air, relieved.

"Your Highness, are you all right?"

I nodded, still shaken from my dream. I couldn't look around very well from my position in his arms. I started to shift.

"You can put me down." He shook his head. His brow was furrowed with concern.

"I'm afraid I can't."

"Why—AHHH!" I yelled. The small amount of shifting that I had done caused pain that shot up from my feet and legs. I held my head up and looked down at them, wincing. My shoes were gone, and my dress had been raised to expose my feet and ankles. They were covered in small cuts that had started to scab over.

"What … hmm … happened?" I asked, clenching my teeth against the pain.

Garen carefully adjusted his arm, which was behind my back, and told me, "When you jumped out from behind me, they launched a large rock at you. It hit the ground at your feet and then exploded into hundreds of fragments. The sound waves that followed caused them to hit your feet. That's where the cuts are from. You fell over and were knocked unconscious when you hit the ground. They stopped firing when you fell. I didn't know what happened to you, nor did your Father, His Majesty. I had started to check on you when the Fizenburg army came over. We are in their camp now."

I glanced above his head and saw red-and-yellow-striped canvas. It was early morning, and the sun was shining through the top of the tent, creating a warm yellow glow. I looked quickly around the tent. Father wasn't there. I glanced at the light coming in again. "How long have I been out? Were you able to ask them why they were trying to hit me?"

"You've been unconscious for just a few hours, Your Highness, and no, I haven't been able to ask." He shifted his arm under my legs, and I winced again. Just then, the tent flap opened, and a man about Garen's height walked in. He was wearing most of his armor, though the chainmail hood and helmet were nowhere to be found. He was maybe in his forties and had streaks of gray starting to show through his black hair. His black mustache was well kept, and the red tabard over the rest of his chainmail bore the Fizenburg crest. A large shield separated into four sections, with some large aquatic animal in the middle that I didn't recognize.

"Is she awake?" His voice was very deep.

"What do you think?" Garen said, with an uncharacteristic snort.

"No need to get upset," the man muttered, frowning.

"No need to get upset?" Garen asked incredulously, raising his eyebrows. I knew that if I didn't say something, the knight or the captain or whoever he was would be arguing with Garen. I pulled my head up from Garen's arm and looked at the man.

"Where's fa—my Griffin?" I was about to ask where Father was but caught myself in time.

A roar sounded just outside the tent, followed by men's shouts. My eyes widened, and I realized Father must have been fighting with some of the knights outside. The man jumped at the sound and then swallowed, trying to regain his composure.

"You mean the thing that was with you, Your Highness? It's being held down by the other guards outside," he replied, pointing to the left.

I furrowed my brow, and he hurried to continue. "It wasn't cooperating. It keeps trying to attack us."

Garen nodded and whispered to me, "His Majesty wouldn't stop fighting long enough to listen to them."

Another roar and snarl was heard outside, followed by more shouts. What was Father trying to do? Get himself and others around him injured? I began to move my foot and then regretted it.

"They haven't hurt it, have they?" I sucked in air while I spoke, and the pain in my feet slowly faded again.

The man shook his head. "No, we are trying to calm it down—"

He was interrupted by a roar just outside the tent flaps. Father lunged into the tent, his rage visible across his entire body. I swallowed and prayed silently that his anger would cool enough for him to listen to reason.

"Annabell! Are you all right?" He came over and looked at my legs.

The knight suddenly jumped in his way and tried to stop him from coming closer.

Father snarled, "Move aside."

The knight didn't move. Another man ran in, out of breath. He was shorter and much younger than the first.

"So … so sorry Sir. We couldn't keep it there." So the knight we had been talking to was a captain. I cleared my throat, and they both turned their heads toward my direction. Father paused. He had been about to push the captain out of the way.

"Thank you for trying to calm my Griffin down. Captain, I would like a moment to talk with my guard alone."

"Of course, Your Highness." The captain gave a slight bow and marched out of the tent, the younger man following him after glancing at Father. When they had gone, Father was still seething.

"Those … those … Do you know they tried to keep me tied up?" He turned his attention to my feet, and some of his anger subsided, "Are you okay?"

I nodded and turned to Garen.

"Set me on Father's back. I should be okay there."

Garen didn't look so sure but, after Father crouched down to make the process easier, he set me there anyway. I sat sideways, my feet swinging slightly and causing a little pain. I gasped and prayed inwardly for the pain to go away. Father stood again and turned his head to face me. He asked me again, "Are you sure you're all right?"

"Yes," I said, releasing the small amount of air I had been holding when I gasped. "I'd like to talk to you about the Fizenburg army. Now don't get upset again before I say more," I said as he opened his mouth, his brow furrowed in anger. "We don't know why they did this so you can't get upset with them quite yet, although I would definitely say an explanation is needed."

I glanced over at Garen, and he nodded his agreement. "This would also be an opportune time to ask to see King Avlin of Fizenburg and ask about the stone and this situation. Please, Father, I prayed that you would calm down enough to listen to reason. I am sure King Avlin would be willing to explain."

Father turned his head back straight and let out a short sigh.

"I am sure you are right. I just want to find your mother without any … All right, I'm willing to listen to what they have to say." He looked at me again and gave me a half smile. "And thank you for praying."

I smiled back and then called out to the captain to return. He entered with a bow and said hesitantly, "I am sorry again, Your Highness, for the trouble we caused. If there is any way we can make it up to you …"

"There is, actually," I said. "Would it be too much trouble—"

65

I was cut off by the same younger knight who had followed the captain out. He came in as I was speaking, with a look of confusion on his face and a letter in his hand. The captain turned to him, annoyed.

"What is it, Puer? You interrupted Her Highness."

Puer gave me an apologetic bow.

"I am sorry, I didn't mean to disrupt." He turned to the captain. "This came for you … from King Avlin."

"What?!"

The young man nodded as the captain took the sealed letter from his hand. He broke the seal and read through it quickly. His expression changed from surprise to confusion. He looked up at me.

"The king wishes to speak to you."

Garen and I looked at each other in surprise. After a moment of silence, I turned to the captain again. "We … we would be glad to speak to King Avlin. Before Puer came in, that was the favor I was going to ask."

He gave me a nod and said, "I will take you to him myself. Come with me." He paused as he lifted the tent flap "Will the Griffin need to stay here?"

Father's voice started to get loud again. "If that …man thinks for one minute I'm staying here, then …" I gently tapped his back to remind him of his promise, and he let out a long breath, calming down again. The Captain jumped at the squawking he heard and nearly dropped the tent flap.

"No. It can come. He's calmed down enough." The captain gave a nervous nod and held the tent flap up higher so I could ride out on Father.

I gently patted the top of my head and quickly pulled it back from the heat. The sun was directly overhead, and it was warming the top of my head. It had taken us all morning, with one stop for a bite to eat, to get through the rolling hills and to Lake Habere. Fizenburg's capital sat on a large island in the middle of the lake, and the only way to get across was by a large bridge. With the noonday sun beating down on us, we began to cross the bridge to Fizenburg, which was twenty feet wide and just under a quarter of a mile long. It was built out of Mollis, a wood that was known for its softness and had a light rusty brown color. I glanced over at Garen. He hadn't said much since we had landed in the hills, and he was now staring quietly ahead of him. I was about to ask him if he was all right when we got to the middle of the bridge. A loud squeaking sound filled the air.

A "Wahoo!" replaced the squeaking, and a few feet from the left side of the bridge, there was a large splash as a creature jumped out of the water. The creature had to be over a hundred feet long and had gigantic flowing fins and dorsal. Its body was blue and shaped like a dolphin's. It leaped over the bridge, laughing loudly, and crashed back into the water on the other side. The waves from both splashes soaked the bridge in front of us.

"Just what we need," the captain muttered. "A Tintta getting the bridge wet." He turned toward us, and I realized that the Tintta was the aquatic creature on the crest. "You'll have to watch your step now. When the Mollis wood gets wet, it releases a gel, making it slippery. Though that was why we used the wood, so that if an enemy tried to cross when it was wet, they would fall."

I saw Father raise his eyebrows and mutter, "More like collapse."

I frowned inwardly. What did he mean? He began to cross the wet section slowly, and he had to dig into the planks with his claws to keep from sliding. Garen was having difficulty too. His boots didn't give him much friction, and he stumbled every so often. Only once, in the thirty minutes it took us to cross the wet section, did he have to support himself on Father.

At the end of the bridge, we were again greeted by the sight of grass. There were only a few trees on the island, along with a few of Fizenburg's cities. The captain led us on a road that bypassed the first two cities and took us directly to the third, which was considered the capital since the castle was at its other end. The city was on the peninsula of the island and was much different than what I had expected. Buildings, some three stories high, lined the streets. The first floors consisted of shops. The upper floors I assumed were living quarters and storerooms for products. The merchants called out to the shoppers to buy their wares, and the smell of spices filled the air. Fizenburg had an economy built on the salt found in the lake, and it had the smell of a fresh breeze. That smell also drifted down the crowded street. As we passed, the merchants' shouts drifted off into silence, and the shoppers stepped to the side of the street. Their gaze followed us, and they didn't speak unless it was in a whisper. The captain snorted at the people's response and quietly chuckled.

"We've never seen a Griffin in this part of the continent, Your Highness. Please don't be offended by their reaction."

Sound erupted in the street when he said Griffin, and again when he said 'Your Highness.' The street stayed parted, and soon after that, we came to the castle gates. I stared at them, amazed, and Garen let out a quiet whistle. They were made of wrought-iron and twisted with swirls and curved to create an image of a Tintta. The captain smiled at our reaction and, after a quick word with the guards, led us in.

The castle was twice the size of our own castle in Misby. The major difference was that the castle was built out of album stone. A white stone that reflected all light and heat. If polished right, it could be used as a mirror. The pale-green roof and banners brought the reflection of the seven towers down to a dull glow. We passed through the courtyard, and the guards up on the wall eyed us warily. The captain led us through the doors to the main hall. It wasn't a very deep hall. Tall floor-to-ceiling windows lined the wall to my right and there were smaller windows on the left. The hall, like the outside of the castle, was built out of the same white stone, and it lit up the room nicely when the light from the windows hit it.

As we entered, I saw a group of men surrounding a man sitting on a throne at the far end. He was glancing over some papers spread out on the table before him. It was King Avlin. He was a taller man, with brown hair so dark it was nearly black. A thin gold circlet rested on his head, glistening from the dim light that came through the windows and the torches. He had a mustache that was thick enough to cover his upper lip. He was wearing a red robe that covered a deep cranberry tunic.

King Avlin looked up from a paper on the table and leaned back in his throne. The men around him, who I assumed were his advisers, stepped back from the table and stood on both sides of the throne. King Avlin, looking displeased, waved a hand, and the table was moved to the side of the hall. He turned his eyes toward the captain. He bowed and said, "Your Majesty, I bring you Princess Annabell of Misby."

He then stood from his bow and stepped to the side of the hall.

King Avlin sat forward with a displeased stare. "Well, Princess Annabell, what are you doing in Fizenburg?"

His voice was low and calculating. I inwardly took a breath and prayed for courage as it was clear that King Avlin was not happy. Still seated on Father, I had to shift slightly to face him. I answered him truthfully, trying to remove all worry and fear from my voice, "We just came to ask to speak to one of your wizards. Just to ask him a question—"

"Why?" King Avlin leaned farther forward, his anger clear, and but his restraint was visible as well. "I have had difficulty with the kingdom of Misby for ten years. At one point, I had to ban their travel into Fizenburg. Now you come to talk to wizards, after what your father did!"

I stared at him, confused, and then glanced at Father. He was staring at the floor.

"Oh, don't tell me you don't know." King Avlin sat back and rubbed his face, his anger starting to fade from it. "It happened when you were ... what? At least five?" He continued when I didn't say anything. "Well, Your Highness, about ten years ago was when my troubles with Misby began. Your father attacked one of my three cities on this island after a trade misunderstanding. Do you realize the damage that was done?"

The anger had left his voice while he spoke, and now he let out a disappointed sigh. Father started muttering but then trailed off. "I am sorry for doing that …" I drew in a breath of realization. That's why Father had said something at the bridge. I sat up straighter.

"Your Majesty … I am sorry for what my father did to you and your cities. If you want us to leave—"

King Avlin held up his hand and shook his head. "You have no need to continue. I have forgiven your father and the rest of Misby. The Lord of heaven and earth reminded me that I am to love my enemies and pray for them. That is why I had repealed the ban of the citizens of Misby not being able to travel or trade here." He sat up straight again.

"I must admit, though, the first couple years after it happened was hard. There was even a wizard who … I'm not sure … was from your kingdom and ready to give service to overthrow your father." To my right, I saw Garen stiffen and then frown.

Father looked up from the ground. I blinked. There had been no wizards in Misby for over a hundred years. King Avlin gave us a confused look. "Is that strange for some reason?"

An adviser to his right leaned closer to the throne. "There have been no wizards in Misby for over one hundred years, sire." The king frowned and looked down at the ground, thinking.

"Your Majesty, do you remember his name?" Garen asked, stepping forward, concerned. King Avlin, still frowning, looked up, "Who are you? Have you been here this entire time?"

Garen bowed, "Yes, sire. I am Her Highness's guard."

King Avlin nodded his head slightly in acknowledgment and then returned to what he had been speaking of before.

"Oh … well, I don't quite remember what his name was." He paused, trying to think. "I believe it started with an *r*. I'm sorry, I don't recall his name."

Still thinking, I asked, "Your Majesty, why were we attacked by the army?" I thought it might have a connection.

King Avlin quickly turned to the captain. "Captain Selverner, what is the meaning … Oh." I looked between the two of them.

"What?" Selverner walked back to the middle of the room

"We had been told, Your Highness, by that same wizard, to shoot down any Griffin with a rider that flew overhead. He had sent a messenger two days ago saying that both would be dangerous to the kingdom."

I looked at Garen, shocked. Who would want to cause us harm? My mind was flashing through the possibilities when Selverner spoke again.

"His Majesty didn't quite trust the wizard. He had us use the flaming rocks to get you out of the sky so he could question you."

King Avlin's frown deepened when he spoke. "I did not order the shatter rock to be used."

I glanced down at my feet. So that was the rock that had caused the cuts. Captain Selverner looked down at the ground.

"No, sire … I will go get the healing ointment." He gave an ashamed bow and left the room. King Avlin waved his hand again, and his advisers followed. When they were gone, he left his throne and came to stand between Garen and me.

"I do apologize for the captain's behavior. I can arrange some visits for you with our wizards." He looked at Father and then at me. "Would you enlighten me, Your Highness, on Griffins? I have never actually seen one." He gestured to Father.

As I began to explain the different types of Griffins, Captain Selverner came back with a small slender glass jar. He bowed when he came over and handed the jar to Garen.

"Just rub some in whenever you feel pain. It will numb the affected area for a few hours, but it should heal and let you walk almost right away."

I smiled and gave him a grateful nod. Garen knelt down and applied the clear gel on my feet. I shifted when he was done to see if I would have any pain, but there was none. I let out a sigh of relief and thanked the Lord in prayer.

King Avlin dismissed Selverner and then spoke. "I understand that no wizards have been in your kingdom for a while. I had one of my advisers send out a message to all of ours to let them know that you would be visiting them the rest of the day. They don't live very far, and there are not many of them, but I am sure that it will take you the rest of the day to talk to them. I would be delighted to have you stay here the for the night and then continue on with your journey tomorrow."

I gave him a nod and gently slipped off of Father's back. "Thank you, Your Majesty. You are very kind."

King Avlin had been right when he said meeting with the wizards would take all day. More often than not, they were too busy thinking about ideas and potential magic that they had to be asked the same question multiple times. Most of them were older gentlemen. Each wizard lived in a different part of the outskirts of the city, and each one lived in a manor. Wizards' manors were not like others. They seemed impossibly tall from the outside, but when you got to the highest story and looked out the window, you would see that they weren't so tall. Most of the wizards, though they were busy, were very kind. However, none of them knew who made the stone.

The stone, they had said, was immune to their magic, or that it was rejecting their spells. We left the last wizard's manor as the sun was setting, and I sighed. We didn't seem to be getting anywhere. There was no place left to search since we had been in all three kingdoms. I had even asked Garen if he knew of any other wizards that lived by themselves. He had said that he did not know, which was a surprise since he pretty much traveled all over the continent. *Lord, show me what to do … I'm lost*, I prayed.

"Is Your Highness ready to return to the castle?" asked Captain Selvener. King Avlin had assigned him to bring us to each of the wizards and also to take us back to the castle. I nodded, and as he led us, a sudden thought popped into my head. I walked closer to Garen.

"Do you find it strange that a wizard from Misby came here?" I asked, looking up at the fading light in the sky.

He kicked a rock that was by his foot and gave a thoughtful nod. "Yes. Considering that we don't have any that I know of. What would be his motive anyway to overthrow His Majesty?"

Father let out a snort.

"Lots of things that I did or didn't do. Who knows?"

I nodded in thought. The wizard could give any reason to overthrow Father, though most of them wouldn't be good ones. What could my father have done to get them so upset? He had been said to be the best king the kingdom had yet. True, he wasn't perfect, but still. I nearly stopped walking when another thought came to mind. Was this the same wizard who had made the stone? Was he also holding Mother captive? *Oh, Mother, where are you?*

CHAPTER

—7—

Queen Casia slowly regained consciousness. The second net that had been thrown over her and Harold was soaked in some liquid with a pungent odor. It had overwhelmed her and caused her to faint. Without even opening her eyes, she could tell that she was on the floor. Her chin was resting on the ground. She moaned and shook her head, the movement not feeling normal. She opened her eyes. Though her vision was not quite clear, she could see that the net had been removed. She could still feel where the net had been, though, as she had nearly rubbed her hands and shoulders raw struggling. When her vision cleared, she found herself in a spacious but very dimly lit room. Objects that she couldn't quite make out were stacked on the far side.

Casia's eyes rather suddenly adjusted to the dim light, and she discovered that the room was round. She lifted her head off the ground, and it went up much higher than she thought it would go. It didn't feel normal. The queen looked down at her arms, which were still on the ground, and screamed. Her arms were gone and replaced by a lion's forearm and paw. Terrified, she sat up and felt something move on her back.

"What ..." She turned her head and gasped. She could turn her head farther than normal. She was looking down her back. Her body had been transformed into a lion's, and two large eagles wings were between her shoulders.

Casia stood and turned in a circle. "What's happened to me? How—" She stopped and looked frantically around. She was alone. "Harold, where are you? Harold? Harold!"

"You're up, I see." Casia froze, and her heart nearly stopped beating. An icy voice suddenly filled the room. It came from everywhere. It had reverberated around the dark room, filling up the spacious place so she couldn't escape from hearing it. It sounded warped, like light coming through glass and being bent. Casia's sight had sharpened with her transformation. No one was in the room that she could see.

"Where are you?" Casia said, her voice just above a whisper. Spinning her head from side to side, she looked around the room. It was silent. Then suddenly, it came again. "You won't be able to find me, Your Majesty. I am not in the room. I have hidden you with much difficulty. You are so well hidden that your husband, and daughter, won't find you for a long time. No one will."

Queen Casia's fear, though still prominent, was overtaken with anger. She growled and began to walk around the room, trying to at least find where the voice was coming from.

"What did you do to them? And me," she hissed as her wings bumped into something.

Whatever it was fell to the ground with a wooden thump. She backed up to the clear space she had been lying in and stayed put. The voice now sounded slightly amused.

"Oh, I did nothing to them. Hm hm, nothing at all, except to persuade them to go looking for you. Ha! And what happened to you? I should think it was obvious by now. You and your husband were turned into Griffins."

"WHAT?! Then where is Harold!?" Queen Casia roared, and the sound of it echoed around the room, almost making her jump.

"He escaped and went to your daughter."

Casia's fear was slowly diminishing, and relief flooded her. Harold was safe, and so was Annabell.

She thought for a second. "Are they looking together?"

"Hm, hm ... yes. And I must say your daughter was ... persuaded very easily to go looking for you." Queen Casia sat back. She narrowed her eyes at the gloom of the room

"You *didn't* turn her into a Griffin, did you?"

"No. Unfortunately." The voice warped again.

Casia started to hiss but then stopped.

"Wait ... if she isn't a Griffin ... How ... how can she talk to—"

"How can she talk to your husband? Oh, has she not told you?" The voice interrupted and mocked. Casia hissed. "Ha! Well your--- precious daughter hasn't told-- anyone that she has a ... special gift."

Casia stopped hissing, and her eyes grew wide as the memory of young Annabell telling her a Griffin spoke came back.

"What ... what do you mean?"

"Well, Your Majesty, your daughter Annabell can talk to creatures."

We had gotten back to the castle, and our rooms were already prepared. Though I lay in bed and tried to relax, I could not. My mind was circulating thoughts and ideas and prayers. Where should we go now? Who was the wizard that came from Misby? And most of all, where was Mother?

I flung the covers off the bed and walked to the window. It was well past midnight, and the moon shone brightly on the landscape. I opened the window and leaned out into the cool wind that greeted me. The gardens were right below the window, and the moonlight gave it a calm and peaceful look. I rubbed my hand over my face and up into my hair. I was worried. Mother could be injured or imprisoned. I was also concerned about the stone. It was still missing, and if it got into the wrong hands ... I rested my head in my hands and leaned on the windowsill.

"Lord, I don't know what to do. Help me please." I stood there silently for a few minutes, listening to the quiet of the night. Then the wind picked up slightly. It came from the direction of Misby. I straightened up as the wind blew through the window, bringing the sound of the chimes. The same ones I had heard when the stone disappeared. I leaned out the window again to hear it clearly.

As I leaned out, a faint whisper suddenly joined the chimes. Where was it coming from? Who was speaking? It was too quiet to hear what it was saying, but it was responding to the chimes. As I listened closely, I realized that the chimes were like words. They would pause, and then the whisper would start in response. I glanced down at the garden, but no one was insight. I looked up again in the direction of the wind. Something came floating into the room. The moonlight caused it to glisten.

As it came into the room, I quickly lit a candle so I could see it more clearly. It was a fine dust. The wind caused it to land on the chest of drawers and begin to pile up. Whenever the chime sound came, the dust that floated by was a rusty gold color. The whisper would change the dust to silver. I stood there for a minute in awe, watching it come into the room.

An idea suddenly occurred to me. Setting the candle on the chest, I quickly went to my satchel at the end of the bed and took out three handkerchiefs. The dust that had settled on the chest's top had separated itself into piles. Using two of the handkerchiefs I grabbed some of each type and laid the two bits of cloth out flat with the third one in between them.

The wind ceased blowing, and the sound of the whispers and chimes disappeared, along with the dust. I gently laid my hand on the two types of dust. First the silver, then the rusty one. I turned my hand over. The dust had stuck and was starting to move across my hand. I quickly, but carefully, placed my hand on the third handkerchief. I removed my hand again and the dust that had come off began to move and intertwine and … glow. A distorted image appeared, and sound came with it. I stared in amazement. I could just make out a female Griffin in a dimly lit round room. Its body was slender, and two thin but sturdy eagle wings were between its shoulders. It had green eyes that looked familiar. And then it spoke.

"What … what do you mean?" I jumped in surprise. It was Mother. I had found Mother! Thank you Lord! But who was she talking to? Her eyes grew wider as if she remembered something terrible, and I became concerned.

"Well, Your Majesty, your daughter, Annabell, can talk to creatures."

I let out a small gasp. The voice! That had to belong to the wizard holding Mother captive. It had to be the wizard, right? It seemed to be the only possibility. I brought my face closer to the image, trying to find where the voice came from. It was also concerning because the voice sounded familiar, but I could not figure out who it was. The image did not show the source of the voice. All it showed was a single room with Mother in it. How had the wizard, who I was pretty sure the voice belonged to, found out my secret? Why had he trapped my mother in a circular room? Where was it? Mother's breathing became labored as realization crossed her face.

"Why? Why didn't I believe her?" She looked down at the floor. I drew in a breath. Mother knew my secret, but I didn't want her to find out about it like this. I wanted to tell her myself. I felt a tinge of annoyance at the wizard, and it made me want to find Mother all the more to explain.

Mother's head suddenly snapped up, confusion and a little bit of anger written across her face.

"Wait … How can you talk to me? Assuming that you are human."

The voice let out a menacing laugh and then spoke.

"Yes, Your Majesty, I am … human. But you should have

guessed by now how I can speak to you. I am a wizard and have been in your husband's service almost since your daughter was born."

I stared at the image, confused. Who was in my father's service that had been there almost as long as I was alive? What was the wizard talking about?

Mother took a step back in shock, and her eyes grew wide again.

"No … you can't be. You're—"

"Yes, Your Majesty, I'm—" the wizard interrupted but cut himself short and then suddenly became angry. "Who's there? WHO'S LISTENING?!" I jumped in surprise. How did the wizard know I had been listening in on the conversation?

A deep red-colored smoke rushed in and filled the room in the image. Mother stumbled and fell over unconscious. The smoke started wafting out of the image. I gasped and quickly blew on the image. The dust flew off the cloth and settled back into its separate piles. I stared wide eyed at the handkerchief, my breath coming out heavily. I had no idea what to think. On one hand, I was relieved that Mother was still alive and all right. But on the other, I was terrified that the wizard's voice seemed to just float about the room. He couldn't be in the room because it was obvious that Mother couldn't find him either. So then how did he get his voice in there?

My breathing returned to normal, and my heart stopped racing. I needed to show this to Father and Garen. I tied the two handkerchiefs closed over their dust and set them in my satchel. I paced again, new thoughts and questions coming to mind. When I did finally go to sleep, I slept only a few hours.

With the little sleep I had gotten, I woke up early. The conversation I had listened in on made me eager not only to leave but also to show Father and Garen what I had found. Garen had already left his room, and Father had stayed in the grand hall to sleep. I walked down the hall of the castle, carrying my satchel, ready to go. The dust was a lot heavier than I expected. It felt like I had placed two large stones in it. The weight caused the satchel to bump against my hip and hindered my pace only slightly. I walked into the grand hall and found King Avlin there, looking around the room in befuddlement and awe.

"What happened here? Who …. some assistance please?" He spun around, looking everywhere. I stopped, and my eyes widened. The already brightly lit stones of the main hall were covered in the rusty gold and silver dust. It not only made the stones brighter, it also made them shine like gems.

Father, who was standing near the door, shook himself after giving an unhappy mutter. A cloud of dust came flying off of him, and maids had rushed in at the king's call and began sweeping the room. King Avlin saw me and came over to me and asked, "Do you know what this is?"

I paused before I answered. Just then, Garen walked in from the other side of the room and caught the king's attention. I gave him a frantic look. I didn't want to tell King Avlin what I had seen.

Garen caught not only my cry for help, but also that I had something that I didn't want to say. He called out as he crossed the room, "What happened here?"

"I don't know myself," King Avlin said, turning to Garen, his hands on his hips.

Father came over and asked Garen, "Do you know what it is?"

Garen bent down and brushed his hand over a pile of rusty gold dust. "It could be just pollen. Or it's mineral dust brought in from the wind." He looked up and Father and the king looked up with him. I followed their gaze. The windows that were near the ceiling for ventilation were open.

The king gave the windows a half frown. "I need to make sure the servants close those." The king turned to me. "Shall I accompany you to breakfast?"

"I would be honored, Your Majesty." We walked out of the grand hall, leaving the maids to finish the cleaning, and into the dining area. The breakfast was delicious, but I hardly noticed it. The thought of the dust was still on my mind. I finished quickly and had to wait for Garen to finish his. I leaned over close to whisper in his ear, "We really should be going. I also have something to tell you."

Garen looked up from his food and then raised his eyebrows with realization. I whispered the same to Father, who was on my right. Garen turned to King Avlin, "Well, we thank you, Your Majesty. It was very kind of you. But we must be going."

King Avlin looked up from his meal with a slight smile on his face. "Oh, you are quite welcome." He turned to me, "I must say, Your Highness, I am glad you were able to stay. When you return home, tell your father I greet him in the Lord."

"Yes, I will," I said, slightly nodding. "We really must be going." I stood, and the satchel bumped into my hip again. The dust seemed to get heavier by the minute. The king stood and bid us farewell and a safe journey, and we were on our way. We got out in the courtyard and mounted Father. He took off into the early morning sky. As we flew, Father began muttering again.

"Well, praise God that the time there was peaceful." He continued this praise and thanksgiving for about a half hour, but I was no longer listening. I was thinking again of the dust. I needed to show it to them. I looked below us. We were flying over the hills again when we had first come to Fizenburg.

Garen tapped me on the shoulder, and I turned to him. "Where are we going now, Your Highness?"

I looked forward again and bit the inside of my lip. I didn't know. The dust didn't show me clearly where Mother was.

Father had overheard Garen's question and replied with a hit of disappointment in his voice, "I can land so we can decide where we are going."

I gave him a nod. "Yes. Please do. I have something to show you both."

By then, we had reached the edge of the rolling hills, and Father started his spiral descent.

Queen Casia shook her head clear and stood up. The deep red smoke that had filled the room had knocked her out again. She didn't like the feeling. She blinked a few times to clear her vision. The voice filled the air again.

"So I see that you have woken up. My smoke was not meant to make you wake up for at least another two hours."

Casia ignored the voice of the wizard. Carefully tucking her wings next to her body, she found it easier to walk around the room. She was worried and afraid. With no visible owner of the voice, it was disturbing. She wanted to get away from it and just have the room be quiet. The horrible voice wouldn't stop its broken speech. Casia began to pray silently to try to calm her thoughts.

Glancing around the room, she realized she could now see more. It was still dimly lit, but more light had come into the room. She could now see the wooden roof and the tower of objects she had originally bumped into. Countless numbers of crates and boxes filled the room like an attic. She was in a tower, she thought, because the roof was built in a cone shape, and there was a trapdoor in the middle of the room where she had been lying. She rushed over to it and tried to pry it open using her beak. It was locked.

"Ah, Your Majesty. You won't be able to escape no matter how hard you try," she hissed, dropping the latch from her mouth.

"WHERE am I? WHY are you doing this? WHERE are you? RELEASE ME NOW!" Her voice didn't echo like the wizard's. It made her slightly angry.

"Temper, Your Majesty. I wouldn't get upset if I were you," the wizard threatened. I had pulled out the handkerchiefs when Father landed and spread them out on the ground.

Garen, who was crouched next to me on my left, was breathing over my shoulder and it started to disrupt the image. I gently pushed him back "Careful, you can't blow on it or it will disappear."

"Oh sorry!" he said and began taking shallow breaths. Father, who was sitting on my right, had landed, but I could tell that he hadn't wanted to. When the image became clear, Father leaned in closer at the sight of Mother. He looked at me and asked "Where is this? Who was that speaking?" I looked at him. Both anger and calmness came across his face.

"I don't know. I do know that the voice is the wizard that King Avlin mentioned. But I am pretty sure she is locked in a tower," I replied.

"You are quite right, listener." My head snapped back the image. The wizard had heard me. Garen and Father leaned in closer and were now both glaring over my shoulders at the image.

Mother turned in a circle, confused. "Who are you talking to now?"

"What?" I muttered.

"Your precious queen is locked in a tower," the wizard continued. "Assuming that you are from Misby and are the same person that listened in last night."

I slapped the grass in front of me. I should have been more careful. The wizard did know that someone had been listening last night, and I hadn't even taken that into consideration when I wanted to show the image to Father and Garen.

The wizard laughed. "Yes, so it was you who was listening in the night before. I don't know who you are yet, but if you get closer to me or the queen that you are trying to save, I will know. And I am sure that you don't want trouble."

A quick bolt of light shot out of the image, and I jerked back to avoid it. Father hissed, and I started to blow on the image. I wanted to silence the wizard, but as the image dissolved, his voice reverberated again and began to chant.

> *Ruts have ridges and hawks have nests; I am one attacked like the rest*
>
> *Ever following his command; I flew from loyalty to my own hand.*
>
> *None of this makes sense, some will say*
>
> *OH! But how it will shed on you knowledge of day*
>
> *Now you have heard me; That is my plan*
>
> *Come and find me if you can!*

Father hissed, and Garen muttered as the dust settled back into its corresponding piles. I had become slightly stunned and scared at the chanting. When I slowed my breathing, I put the handkerchiefs back in my satchel. Garen got up off the ground.

"Ruts have ridges …" He scratched his head, thinking. "Is the wizard … talking about a place?" Father frowned and shook his head as he raised it.

"I don't think so. That chant has clues in it, yes, but I don't think the first line is a place. It makes absolutely no sense."

Garen nodded. "I didn't understand what you said, Your Majesty, but I agree with you completely."

I smiled inwardly and stood up, temporarily taken away from present matters. Throughout our journey, Garen had become amazingly good at guessing what Father said. I didn't know if he was guessing from the sounds he was hearing or something else. The thought of the chant crossed my mind again. It reminded me of what King Avlin had said. The wizard showed up after Father had attacked one of Avlin's towns. Was there any connection with the line in the poem? Another idea suddenly came to mind.

Turning, I asked, "Garen? Do you know someone who is really good at solving riddles?"

Garen *had* traveled almost everywhere on the continent, and he knew a lot of people. He thought for a moment and then pointed back to Fizenburg. "Well, I do know someone. Lord Vermue, the last wizard that we met in Fizenburg. He should be able to help. If you and His Majesty wouldn't mind going back, we can ask him."

I sighed. Going back would mean that it would take longer to solve the riddle and find Mother. I looked over at Father, and he gave a slight nod. We had no other choice. There was no other way to solve what the voice had said.

"All right. Let's go."

CHAPTER

— 8 —

Lord Vermue's manor was the farthest from Fizenburg's cities. It was past noon when we reached his door. When I slid off Father, I noticed a change. His wings slightly sagged, and his face was downcast. I came over to his head.

"Father?"

He swallowed. "Annabell … I … I'm losing hope." Tears formed in his eyes, and he sat down with his head lowered. "It has taken longer than I expected to find her … What if it's too late?"

I put my arms around his feathered neck and hugged him. I whispered quietly, trying to keep myself from crying, but tears came anyway, "Oh, Father. We will find her. God will help us. He provides. I know he will." I looked into his eyes. "I've learned that from you."

We stood there for a moment, just embracing. Father took a slow deep breath and nodded to Garen, who stood by the door waiting. As Garen used the large brass knocker, Father turned to me with a small smile.

"Thank you." I just smiled in return and then looked at the wizard's large manor doors. They were made of the Mollis wood like the bridge and carved with intricate aquatic designs. The manor itself was large, just like many others. High windows stretched from the ground to the roof in one part, indicating that there was a large gathering room. The house was multiple stories high, and few of the windows had balconies. It was made up of the same stone as the castle. Large pillars of album stone stood on either side of the entrance, holding up the red-tiled roof. The door on the right opened, and there stood the wizard we had seen just yesterday.

"Yes? Hello, Garen, Your Highness. What can I do for you?" he asked. He was a shorter man and had a gray beard that nearly reached the ground. The man's hair was gray, except for the thinning spot at the back of his head.

Lord Vermue's voice was a direct contrast to his age, as he sounded to be in his midthirties. He had a cheerful smile on his face, but his aged hazel eyes were filled with concern and alarm. He wore a robe that hung on him like a cloak. It was white and embroidered with the gold design of the Fizenburg crest.

Garen, noticing the concern in Vermue's eyes, returned the wizard's smile. "Hello, Lord Vermue. We have something that we need your help with."

The wizard's smile suddenly faded from his face. He opened the door just a little wider, "Come in quickly."

Father hesitated.

"The Griffin too."

Once we were inside, he quickly closed the door. It nearly slammed shut in the process.

I turned to Lord Vermue. "What's the matter?" He didn't answer. He locked the door and ushered us into a large sitting room. The walls were covered in a light brown wood, and there was a red carpet covering the floor. The floor-to-ceiling windows we had seen outside spanned the length of the far wall. Three chairs had been set up next to a very big fireplace with a table in between them.

"Won't you sit down?" Lord Vermue said hurriedly, and he closed the door into the room. Garen and I looked at each other. What was he doing? We hesitantly sat down in two of the chairs, and Father sat next to me on my left. Garen was on my right, closer to the fireplace. Only when Lord Vermue was seated in the chair opposite of all three of us did he speak again.

"I am glad you came back to me quickly. I know why you have come. Don't ask me how—it will take too long to explain." He held up his hands in defense when I opened my mouth. He lowered his hands and began to gently roll them over each other anxiously, "I have been waiting for you." He glanced hastily at the large windows and decided to shut the curtains.

"Why were you waiting for us? Does that mean ... you can help us?" I asked as each curtain closed with a *whoosh*. The room dimmed only slightly as one of the white stone walls was still exposed and reflected torch light. Lord Vermue came and sat back down on the edge of his seat. I gave him a concerned look. What was wrong?

"Yes, Your Highness, I can help ... but not in the way you might think. I can tell you some things, but not others." He wrung his hands together and glanced at me and then Garen and finally Father, "Mostly for the sake of Garen and Your Highnesses protection. Along with King Harold." I blinked

"How did you know that this is my..." Lord Vermue shook his head

"I have no time to explain. Will you tell me how you came to understand that the wizard captured Her Majesty? I need to know as much as I can to help you."

Slightly startled by the question, I told Lord Vermue what happened with the dust and the image that it created when swirled together.

"Can you tell us what the riddle means?" Garen asked after I had finished.

When I told it to Lord Vermue, his eyes widened, and he now turned them to Garen.

"I fear that if I tell you outright, more harm will be caused. Particularly, more trouble, as the wizard will be able to find how you solved it. I can tell you one thing about it, though, to help you decipher it. The riddle is more of a poem than a riddle. It's what is called an acrostic."

I sat there for a minute, thinking over the poem. Garen's face was blank, but my eyes widened, and Father began to mutter.

I barely whispered, "It spells something."

Lord Vermue nodded, and Garen looked at me, confused. I turned to him and spoke quickly. "An acrostic is a certain type of poem. The first letter of each line spells out a word."

Garen's eyes brightened with realization.

I turned toward Lord Vermue. "Can we write it out?"

He gave no reply but handed me a sheet of paper and a quill that he just pulled out of his sleeve. I took the paper and quill from him and knelt down at the table that was between the group of chairs and started writing each line. As I wrote, I asked, "Can you tell us what each line means as well?"

Lord Vermue stood and watched on my right. "I can only help you understand. I can't tell you the answer."

"That is all right, sir," Garen said, coming to kneel next to me. "Just help us to find what we are missing." I finished writing the poem and began to read it aloud.

"'Ruts have ridges, Hawks have nests; I am the one attacked like the rest.'"

Lord Vermue looked at Father. "What did the king of Fizenburg tell Annabell?"

Father gave him a concerned frown. "That I had attacked one of his cities over a trading misunderstanding."

I opened my mouth to repeat what Father had said, but Lord Vermue just nodded. I stared at him and then shook my head. He was a wizard. Of course he could understand Father. I turned back to the poem.

"So the wizard was from the town that was attacked?" I guessed.

Lord Vermue gave me a slight nod.

"This house is actually built on the location where it used to be. I had lived there before it was destroyed."

Father gave him an apologetic look. "I'm sorry for that. I pray that you will forgive me, sir."

Lord Vermue waved his hand. "I bear no grudge, Your Majesty," he said, then urged Garen to read the next line.

"'Ever following his command, I flew from loyalty to my own hand.' So wait … 'following his command' … was the wizard working for His Majesty?"

I thought for a minute and then nodded. "He had to be because King Avlin said the wizard came from Misby, and last night, I heard that he had been in Father's service just before I was born." I looked at the rest of the poem.

The rest of it just seemed like filler to complete the spelling. Garen was still thinking. He stood and helped me off my knees. "Do you know who was around at the palace that time?"

I thought for a minute, and then my breath caught in my throat. There was only one person I could think of. Father began to growl as he realized it too. I looked at the poem.

"Oh no," I whispered.

Lord Vermue remained silent, but he could see that I had found the answer.

"What's the matter, Your Highness?"

I showed Garen the poem. "Read the first letters."

"R-E-N-O-N?" Garen said each letter but left out the last line when he realized who it was. Anger spread across his face as he said it again.

"Renon!" Father yelled in rage. The sound shook the house, and Garen almost pulled his sword out of its sheath.

Father was furious. He pushed through the sitting-room doors and back out to the front entrance. As he left, a burst of light seemed to fill the room, as though his anger was becoming visible. Not wanting him to leave without me or Garen, I quickly stuffed the paper and quill into my satchel. I turned to thank Lord Vermue, but he was gone. I glanced around quickly as Garen started to leave. Where had he gone?

"Your Highness, we must go."

I had no more time to look. I ran after Garen, trying to keep from tripping on my dress. I yelled as loud as I could, thinking the house could carry my voice to him if he was in another room.

"Thank you! We really appreciate it!" I rushed outside, with Garen close behind. Father had nearly taken off.

"Wait!" I called out.

He hurriedly lowered himself, muttering so quickly that I could not understand him. Garen practically tossed me up onto Father's back. No sooner had we sat down than Father leaped off into the sky. I leaned into Father's back, willing him to fly faster. I was angry. Why had Renon done this? Just because Father had attacked one of Fizenburg's cities didn't give him much of a right to try to kidnap my parents. What did he plan to do with Mother? Where was she even being kept prisoner?

Garen started to mutter. "I never liked him. What does he plan—"

The rest of his speech was cut off as Father's flying speed increased. His resentment and urgency fueled his flight. The wind rushed past, drowning out the sound, and after a while, the strength of my anger did as well. Concern and worry came over me as I remembered that we would be discovered if we came closer. Was there any way to find out where Mother was and rescue her without Renon knowing?

At the thought of him, I frowned. I had disliked Renon when we left. But he had insisted that I did not go on this journey, hadn't he? Why hadn't he wanted me to leave? Then suddenly, everything from the beginning of the journey came flooding back into my mind and fell into place. The fake invitation, the planned carriage crash, the ambush. He had set it up and didn't want me to go and uncover his plot. My brow furrowed in anger, and I ground my teeth together. After what he had done, I not only disliked him, I was angry at him.

I glanced over at the sun. It was starting to sink below the horizon. With Flying Arrow Woods in front of us, we passed over the last of the rolling hills. Banking to the left, Father avoided the forest and went north in the direction of Misby. The sky turned a frost blue, and the mountains around Misby came into sight on the horizon. As the distance between us and home shortened, Father increased his speed again, anxious to return and, no doubt, give Renon a piece of his mind. The sun sank lower, and the sky turned purple.

Queen Casia was tired. She was tired of a lot of things—tired of waiting, tired of being in a small room, tired of the whole ordeal. It had been hours since the voice had stopped talking to … whoever it was, wherever they were. Giving a frustrated sigh, Casia stood and began to walk about the room again. There was not much else to do and no way to escape. The tower's room was not very large. It had no windows, and it made the space feel smaller. Without an outside view, there was no telling where the tower was built. The voice laughed

"Are you bored, Your Majesty?"

Queen Casia hissed. "Renon, if you don't let me out—"

"On the contrary, you should be the one concerned. Remember, I am a wizard."

Casia yelled in frustration and knocked over a pile of crates in front of her. They fell, and one of the lids came off, spilling the box's contents. A sheet of paper floated to the floor. It was a child's drawing of a Griffin signed with the messy name: "Annabell." Casia stared at it. She was home, in the castle's tallest tower. No one hardly ever went up here as the space was used as an attic. She stared at the drawing. It was not a very good representation of a Griffin. Casia nearly cried. Why hadn't she believed her daughter? Would she ever see Annabell or Harold again?

A breeze came from behind the boxes she had knocked over. She looked up. That was strange. Queen Casia followed it, confused. A windowless tower that had a breeze? Gently shoving the toppled boxes aside, she followed the breeze. It came from a crack in the stone wall, and near it was a large dome-shaped object. It had been covered in a thin red material, and the edges, which hung just above the ground, had a rusty gold embroidery of owls and other intricate designs. Casia stared at it, confused. When had this been put here?

Renon's voice suddenly sounded from beneath the cloth.

"What do you think you are doing?"

Dust flew off the embroidery and around Casia. She hissed at his voice and then regarded the cloth. Renon couldn't be hiding beneath it. It wasn't shaped right. What was beneath it, then? She snagged the edge of the cloth and slid it off the object. It dropped to the ground, and the rusty gold dust blew in every direction from the embroidery, making her sneeze. Underneath the cloth was the largest glass ball Casia had ever seen. It was waist high, and its sides were blown perfectly smooth. It sat on a low-sloped cone. The inside was hollow and filled with a red mist. Rusty gold sparks moved with the mist, and owl shapes swirled together. It was beautiful. She stared at it, mesmerized. Suddenly, Renon's scowling face appeared in the mist.

"I see you found the glass."

Casia growled, "When did you put this here? How are you looking through it?" She circled the sphere. Renon wasn't there.

"The glass ball around my neck. I enchanted it to become a viewing glass."

"So you could keep an eye on me."

"Yes, though sound doesn't travel through glass well." Casia glared. This glass ball was what released Renon's voice. The warped sound was produced because of it. She wanted to get rid of it. Still glaring, she looked up at the ceiling. An idea occurred to her. Renon saw her look up.

"If you do any—" Casia's anger moved through her body, and she roared. Leaping upon the glass ball, she grasped it between her paws. She flew to the ceiling, climbing higher and higher with it. The ceiling was much farther from the floor than she expected, and it only whittled her idea into shape more.

Renon yelled through the glass, "I'm warning you …,"

Casia snarled, "I don't care to listen to you!" She released it. It sank through the air, its weight causing it to gain more and more momentum. When it finally hit the ground, a thunderous explosion shook the tower, and Casia faltered in her flight. A burst of light shot up from the ground, and she barely dodged it. The red mist inside expanded and then …

"I told you."

Queen Casia looked down. She shrieked in fear and rage. Right in the middle of the glass fragments and dust was Renon. He was staring up at her; his scowl had deepened.

"That could have been your biggest mistake."

We were not that far away from the castle when the sun set. The stars were out, and they were dancing across the night sky. It was nearly impossible to see where we were going. I sighed. I knew Father was going to hate this suggestion, but … "Father?" I said, leaning forward. "We need to land. We can hardly see where we're going, and we need a plan."

Father, whose anger had subsided some with flight, let out a frustrated groan. "I know, but I would like to keep going."

Garen leaned up next to my back so he could be heard. "Your Majesty, it would be in our best interest to land. Like Her Highness said, we can create a plan, and you can also rest."

That got him. I could tell he was tired. At the mention of rest, he started his descent. He landed next to a spring and river that was less than a hundred miles away from Misby. We still had a ways to go, but we were not far. Garen slid off, and I followed him. Sleep suddenly tugged at my consciousness.

"This is terrible," I said with a yawn. "What are we going to do?" My eyelids drooped, and my satchel began to bounce against my hip, making me stay awake. Garen sat on the ground, looking exhausted and upset.

"You know, before we left, I heard something behind the grand hall doors. That was probably Renon watching us leave. I never liked him." My satchel suddenly swung out to arm's length and began to sway. Garen, who jumped up, and Father both stared at it.

"What is going on," I said, my brow furrowing. I carefully lifted the flap, and instantly, a small orb of light shot out. It nearly hit me in the face, and would have if I didn't dodge it. I let out a yelp of surprise and stumbled backward. It was the size of a coin, and it gave off a warm golden glow. After hovering for a few seconds, it danced around my head and did the same to Garen. It dove around and wove in and out of Father's legs. He swiped at it, annoyed. The light dodged his paws and tail, and then just as suddenly as it had started moving, it stopped. Landing on the ground, the orb slowly became bigger and bigger. Its brightness increased and lit the surrounding trees. When the light faded, in its place was an owl. Not just any owl but my pet owl. William.

CHAPTER
— 9 —

I stared at him. Sleep had given up on tugging at my consciousness, and now amazement was running around.

"What are you doing here?!" I asked, almost yelling. For one thing, I thought that he was still at the castle. Second, *how* exactly had he gotten into my satchel? And how had he become a bright light? I knelt down.

"I'm here to help ... and to apologize," William said, opening and refolding his wings. His voice was sort of quiet but had a soft sound to it. He was a snowy white color with tan wingtips and a tan pattern on the top of his head. Garen and Father both stared at him.

Garen pointed. "Wha ... he ... how? He can talk?" he finally said.

I stared at Garen.

"You can understand him?"

Both he and Father nodded. How was that possible? I stood again, trying to think. Did William have the ability to speak aloud? If so, how?

"Garen, would you mind making a fire so we could have a little more light?" I asked, still trying to figure out what had happened.

Garen, still staring wide eyed at William, began to gather wood from the surrounding trees. William ignored him and flew onto my shoulder, a position he normally took when I was at home.

"Like I said, Your Highness, I am sorry. I was the one who told Renon what you could do." He lowered his head, ashamed.

I rubbed my hand over my face. This was disturbing. Finding out that I had an animal that could talk to people was not something I expected to hear. I tried to focus on what he had been saying and then became wide eyed when I realized what he had said.

"You … you told him?"

He nodded. My memory flashed back to the afternoon I tried to tell Mother the Griffin had spoken. William had been sitting there watching me argue with Mother. When Mother had left, after firmly telling me that Griffins could not talk, I went over and told him what I had heard. There was a sharp crack that brought me back to the present. Garen had lit a fire and snapped a branch to throw in. Both he and Father were watching it and glancing my direction every so often. I frowned at William.

"Why did you tell him?" The light reflected off of his eyes giving him a sorrowful look.

"I don't have the liberty or the time to explain. I am sorry. To show you that I am sorry, I would like to help. Your Highness, quickly, you must use the dust."

I blinked as he flew back to the ground. Garen and Father both looked up at him from the fire with a start.

"How did you know—?"

He cut me off. "You will eventually find out how I have come to know things. But, Your Highness, you must use it."

"I don't know if I should, though," I said, but I took it out anyway. "Renon can find out who is listening because we are so close." William nodded and gave a quick look around.

"It's okay. When I am looking with you, he will see only me."

I knelt over by the fire so I could see and began pulling out the three handkerchiefs I had been using. Father and Garen came over as William hopped to my side. I stared at him for a second and then began to mix the dust. The quick look he gave reminded me of someone we had met, but I couldn't remember who. The firelight caused the dust to sparkle and glow brightly as the image appeared.

William leaned over the image, not blocking my view but covering most of it. I gasped as the image finished forming. Renon was in the room with Mother. When did he get there? What was he doing? Garen and Father both growled in anger. The dust showed that Mother was up in the air and Renon was on the floor, surrounded by broken glass. What had been broken? He was scowling up at Mother so hard it nearly made me scream.

"That could have been your biggest mistake." Mother hissed, the anger visibly written across her face,

"What could you possibly do to me?" Renon opened his mouth to reply, giving her sneer, but Mother interrupted before he could say anything.

"No, never mind … I don't want to know. And besides, you're stuck here now as well." Renon raised his left arm up to the ceiling, and light started come off his fingertips

"You keep forgetting, Your Majesty. I AM A WIZARD!" His voice caused the handkerchief to vibrate and the image nearly disappeared. Light began to come out of his hand when Renon paused and narrowed his eyes. He glanced around the room angrily,

"Who's listening? I warned you …" He paused and looked right through the image at me, and I flinched

"William! How did you know how to listen in?" he yelled, lowering his hand. I held my hand to my chest and let out a breath of air, remembering that he couldn't see me.

Renon continued, "You useless bird! Where are you? Have you done what I asked?"

William looked down into the image with such a frown that I nearly laughed. Seeing an owl frown looks hilarious, but now was not a time to laugh.

"You'll know later," he said in an irritated voice. He glanced up at me and then looked back to the image. "I need to know where you are. I am coming back."

Mother, who was still in flight, began to circle the room. She paused and looked right out of the image as well.

"What are you looking at? Who are you talking to?" Renon ignored her and pointed through the image. His frown didn't disappear.

"You know perfectly well where I am, you useless bird. And if you bring anyone with you I will personally kill you."

"No, I don't think you will." William let out a snort, gave Renon a smile as though he knew something he didn't and quickly waved his wing over the dust, causing the image to dissolve and scatter in every direction. He stalked a few steps away from the fire and let out a *Hmph*. I turned to him after I put the dust away.

"Do you know where they are?" He looked at me over his shoulder,

"I do, but I had asked that to show you I was trying to help."

"What was it that he wanted you to do?" Garen asked skeptically. I turned to look at him. He was standing near my right shoulder with his hand hovering over the hilt of his sword. William turned back toward us and gestured toward Father.

"He wanted me to find His Majesty and make sure that he could not get back." He didn't look too happy and was a little concerned that he had said anything at all.

Father hissed and took a threatening step toward him. William didn't move, but he hurried to continue.

"But I don't want to. Not after all that he has done to cause problems for your family and all the problems I've had with him. Now regarding your question again, Your Highness," he said, turning to me, "I do know where Her Majesty is and will tell you exactly where you can find her."

My eyes widened. Garen's arm dropped from his sword, and his mouth fell open. Father was instantly upon him. He leaped past both Garen and me and stood right over William.

"Tell me *now*. Where. Are. They." His breath was coming out hard as he tried to keep his anger in check.

William didn't flinch but calmly took a step back and out from under Father.

"They are, at this moment, in the topmost tower of the Misby castle." I jumped to my feet as Father and I yelled, "WHAT?!"

Garen added, "She's been here the entire time?!"

William nodded and began to rub his wings together. There was that movement again. Who was it that was so familiar? Father roared and turned to fly, but I stopped him by touching his side.

"Wait! Father! You can't just go and expect to get Mother back! Renon won't listen!"

He lowered his wings and gave an unhappy growl and began raking the turf beneath him with his claws. I prayed again that his anger wouldn't get the best of him.

He looked up at me after a minute or two. "I know, but I am just too worried for her. How are we going to do this?"

I shook my head. "I don't know. Fighting a wizard will definitely not be easy." I looked over at Garen.

"We should get Lord Vermue. He helped us before." Garen said.

I nodded in agreement, and out of the corner of my eye, I saw William ruffle his feathers in sudden excitement. "I can send him to the castle as soon as you say the word, Your Highness."

I gave him a thoughtful nod. "All right. Hopefully, he won't be too nervous to help. If we get into the castle, Fedren and the rest of the guards can help us." Father was anxious and sat with his tail in constant motion,

"We should also pray about all of this."

I nodded, and so all four of us stood in a circle and talked to the Lord. We asked him to give us wisdom in what to do and to grant my father peace so that he could think clearly and to give us the help that we needed. When we finished with an "Amen," William slowly began to rub his wings together again. I blinked as I remembered who the motion reminded me of. William's mannerisms reminded me of Lord Vermue himself. I turned to him.

"William, would you do me a favor?"

"Yes, Your Highness," he said, giving me a nod.

"Will you please go get Lord Vermue and send him here now? You can get to him faster than any of us."

He smiled and spread his wings. "Your Highness, he knows you need help. He is on his way to the castle right now." William turned and flew in the direction of the castle.

I raised my eyebrows. Lord Vermue already knew? I shook my head, confused, and turned to Garen and Father. "I think it would be best to stay the night here."

"All right, but I fear sleep will be a long time in coming," Father sighed and lay down.

"His Majesty is right," Garen said, kicking dirt over the embers of the fire to put it out.

"I know, but we have to get whatever sleep comes our way," I muttered as sleep again started to tug at my consciousness. I sat down next to Father and rested my head against his side with a sigh, wishing that the night would end. Garen soon followed, and seconds later, I drifted off to sleep to the sound of Father's breathing.

CHAPTER
— 10 —

Casia glared down at Renon. He had turned his attention back to her after he stopped talking to whoever it was. Glaring at her, he raised his hand again

"Now, back to you, Your Majesty." He started muttering, and light launched out of his raised hand. It shot toward her and went flying over her head as she dove to try to avoid it. When the light hit the ceiling, it exploded into a shower of sparks.

Casia's anger was still overriding her fear, and because of it, she dove at him. Shrieking, she tried to grab him but he ducked and shot another spell. Casia dived again. This time she managed to latch on to the back of his robe, but it ripped as she tried lifting him into the air. Renon stumbled to the floor. He rolled and stood up before Casia could come at him again

"You think that by attacking me I can be stopped?" he hissed, picking himself up. "You haven't even seen the worst of my power!"

Fear began to overtake the anger that had been flowing through her mind. No longer attacking him, she furiously flew around the room, trying to stay out of his grasp. Because of her flight, Casia didn't see that Renon was preparing another spell. Reaching into his pocket, Renon grabbed something and threw it into the air. A small red ball with a black stone in the center came zooming toward her. She dodged it easily, but as she let out a triumphant "Ha!," it hit the ceiling above her. It exploded, causing her to falter in flight, and released a cloud of red mist that completely engulfed her.

Casia flapped her wings, desperately trying to get away, but it followed her. The more she flapped, the thicker it became. It was so thick that she could no longer see through it. Seconds later, she found that she could not move. She was frozen and hovering in midair.

Renon laughed. "And now, Your Majesty," he said, moving his hands in a pulling motion. The cloud came to him with Casia trapped inside "You get your wish."

The sun had come up over the mountains hours ago. We all had woken up at the crack of dawn and begun the flight back to the castle. We had been flying for two or three hours, and were not much farther from the castle. Being just under a hundred miles from finding Mother gave Father speed. But the journey still took time. We were within sight of the castle when we flew over a small hill, close enough to see it but not clearly.

I glanced around the village and the forest, hoping to see William with Lord Vermue. They were nowhere in sight, and my shoulders sank, realizing that William might be longer in coming than I thought. I thought back over our travels as we came to the forest before the castle. It had now been roughly nine days since I left. I hadn't realized it had been that long until Garen mentioned it when we left the stream this morning. I looked toward the castle and shivered.

Usually, if Mother and Father went on a trip, I would be in charge and make sure that the castle ran smoothly. But since I wasn't there, and neither were my parents, Renon was in charge, as he was my Father's adviser. That's what made the situation worse than before. I shivered again at the sight of the castle. He had changed so much without changing the castle. How he could change my home that much in just nine days, I did not know. The castle looked darker and more guards were posted than normal. The flags had not been changed, but they seemed entirely different. I looked at our tallest tower. We were almost flying eye level, even with the distance we still had to go. It was the perfect place to hide Mother. There were no windows at the top or up its sides. I tried to remember the last time anyone had been in it. Nothing came to mind.

I leaned forward to talk to Father. "Why do we even have that tower if we don't use it?"

Father shrugged.

My thoughts again returned to William. "Do you think William will be back in time?" His shoulder came up, paused, and then went down.

"I don't know. I don't trust him very well yet. He just suddenly decides to help us? That's strange, if you ask … me." His last sentence was slurred, and I frowned. Garen tapped my shoulder.

"Your Highness? What is wrong with His Majesty?" I looked at Father again. Something was wrong. He looked like he was struggling. His flaps became less constant. His wings would flap and then pause, like they were freezing up.

"Father, please land!" But there wasn't much choice. Father's wings gave one last pump before we plummeted. We were even closer to the castle now, but not close enough to be seen. Father nearly crashed as we fell through the trees, but he evened himself out before hitting the ground.

I was thrown off Father's back, and Garen followed, but he was able to catch me and righten both of us in the process. Father lay on the ground uncomfortably still, frozen.

I rushed to his side, afraid of the worst, and turned and motioned to Garen.

"Come help—"

Father suddenly roared in pain. "ANNABELL! Help!" He suddenly began moving. He stood up, and his wings flared. Then he collapsed again and began to thrash about on the ground. Scared, I wanted to help but had no idea of what to do. Father kicked and flared his wings, and I jumped, trying to stay out of the way.

"Father! What is it? What's wrong? Father!" I yelled, trying to come closer to help, but Garen held me back. A sudden red mist enveloped him. Light shot out in every direction. Garen and I dropped to the ground to avoid it, and then it disappeared. The mist lingered and then dissipated entirely. When it vanished, I gasped.

There, lying propped up on his arm, dazed, was Father. He was no longer a Griffin. I let out a cry of joy and rushed to him and knocked him over as I hugged him.

"Father! Oh, my father! You're back! You're back."

"Annabell, my love, my child!" He hugged me back, and we both sat up, embracing each other and crying.

Casia woke up again for the third time. She had passed out from the mist and didn't remember what had happened after she froze. She shook her head to clear her vision and realized that the room had changed. For one thing, there was more light. The boxes that had been surrounding her were all piled on one side of the tower. There was a window, which was outlined by curtains and had never been there, in the wall not far from her. It was about two or three hours into the day as the sun was not visible out the window in the blue sky. With the sun risen, plenty of light came into the room.

Casia looked around. Things had been added that were not there before. A large fireplace with a tapestry hanging over it was on the left side of the room, opposite the boxes. There was furniture too. She sat up and found that she had been lying on a sofa. She saw Renon facing the fire, his back to her. Looking around the room,

Casia again saw the trapdoor. As quietly as she could, she stood, and her head began to swim. She touched her head, trying to regain her balance before she continued on. She felt different. She lowered her hand and stopped. Her hand. Surprised at this, she screamed, forgetting to be silent.

Renon turned around. His voice was mocking. "Surprised, Your Majesty? Have the things I added upset you?"

Casia stood up. She was a human again. The dress she had been wearing the day the carriage was attacked was on her now. The only difference was that it was slightly soiled and wrinkled from her struggle getting out of the carriage. Although happy that she was no longer a Griffin, she turned angrily to Renon.

"What do you want? You … you monster! You have had your fun with me by keeping me here. What are you planning to do?"

Renon scowled and crossed the room in two strides, getting within inches of Casia's face. He grabbed her forearm and whipped her around. She let out a yelp of pain and he sneered.

"If you're so interested, I'll tell you. I want to rule Misby. It may come as a shock to you," he said, shoving her back onto the sofa, "but I am not from Misby. I am from Fizenburg."

Casia's mouth dropped open as she massaged her arm.

"Yes, that's right. I came to work here, and King Harold chose me as his adviser. Your husband, or should I say His Majesty, destroyed the town that my soon-to-be wife and family was living in. Do you realize what that did to me? It broke my heart that I would not see my love again." His anger drained from his face, and in a fleeting moment, Casia saw grief. But in the next moment, the anger returned, and he glared at her.

"I was so angry that when I found out, I rushed to the king of Fizenburg thinking that I would get assistance to destroy King Harold and his kingdom. But he denied me that service. He didn't want to cause more problems. So from that time, I set out to become a wizard. Watching and waiting for the perfect time."

He paused to take a breath and began to yell, "I was the one that sent you the invitation to draw you away. I was the one who enchanted the carriage to burst into flame. I was the one who enchanted a stone that would make you turn into Griffins. I was the one that hired men from Flying Arrow's Woods to capture you."

Horror filled Casia. She stared at him—confused, afraid, and angry.

"You? You did all of this?" Her anger mounted, and she stood up. "And what about my husband? What have you done to him? You're such a coward you can't even perform magic in front of him!"

Renon just laughed, and it caused Casia to fall back onto the sofa.

"I just changed him like I changed you. That was part of the enchantment I planned. When one of you changes, the other changes with them. I was hoping that he was up in the air when I changed you back."

Casia gasped and glared at him

"How could you? You sneaking, conniving—"

"Careful, Your Majesty." Renon held up his hand, and sparks flew off his fingertips. A very deep frown formed on his face. "You don't want to lose your temper again, now, do you?" He took a step toward her, and she jumped off the sofa and went to the middle of the room.

Suddenly, wind blew through the window, and both turned their gaze toward it. Casia stared at it. Why hadn't she thought of escaping through the window? She could … She stopped herself. Now that she was human, she couldn't use the window. She wouldn't be able to fly away. The wind blew again, and it regained Casia's attention.

A strange sound came floating in. The sound of gigantic wings. And then, just as suddenly as the sound came, it was silent. Casia's heart was beating hard. Was it Harold? *Oh please, Lord,'* she silently prayed, *'don't let it be him. Please don't let harm come to him.*

Renon frowned and rushed to the window. "Was that … No, I don't see anything." He started to turn away but then turned back.

"Oh, it's William." His frown deepened again "About time he showed up! Why is he always late? How does he manage …"

The rest of his speech was muffled as a full-grown owl flew through the window. He looked rather friendly. His feathers were snowy white, with tan wingtips and a tan cluster of feathers on the top of his head.

"Greetings, Your Majesty, Renon," he addressed them both and nodded.

Casia stared. The owl could talk? This was what Renon had been talking to? William had landed in between Casia and Renon and was giving Renon the most discontented look. Renon took a step away from the window toward him.

"Have you found them? Did you prevent him from returning?" He did not look utterly happy.

The owl shuffled its wings and stared back at him.

"Yes, I have found them."

"Where are they?"

When William didn't respond, Renon's hand began to spark again at his side

"Don't test my patience, William--"

"Wait, you're William?" Casia cut in. The name had caused a memory to come up in her mind. She continued, "The owl we found for Annabell?"

William nodded. "I am, Your Majesty." Casia was about to ask another question when Renon hissed and sparks crackled out of his hands,

"Silence! Do you have any idea who you are dealing with?"

Casia swallowed her words and shut her mouth.

William took a few steps back and was now closer to Casia. He didn't look worried at all.

"On the contrary. Do you know who you are dealing with?"

The wind rushed into the room again, wiping everything

around. The tapestry flew up from the wall, the curtains near the window twisted wildly, and Casia's dress spun about her legs. A gold-colored mist enveloped William, and there was a burst of light. The wind faded and took the mist with it.

Casia gasped. In the place of the owl was a man not much shorter than Renon. His hair was gray and thinning at the top of his head. His beard nearly reached the floor and was streaked with gray. He was in a white robe embroidered with gold.

Renon took a step back in horror. His voice came out in a low whisper and then grew louder.

"Vermue? No, NO! It can't be you!"

The man nodded, and Casia stared wide eyed at him. Vermue took a step toward Renon.

"Yes, it is me, brother."

Renon let out a howl of rage and lifted his hand. "NO!"

Rusty gold dust, sparks, and lightning flew toward Vermue. He ducked, and it hit the pile of boxes behind him. Pulling Casia to his side, he thrust his hands flat, up into the air. A gold-tinted force field enveloped him and Casia. His palms supported the top of the dome like a shield. Renon howled.

Vermue turned to Casia, who stood frozen, stunned. "Your Majesty, you need to escape. I can't hold this shield forever. Go." He pointed to the trapdoor, and a beam of light shot out of his finger. "The door is unlocked and open."

Casia fell out of her trance and looked around. The trapdoor was inside the shield. As she rushed toward it, it sprang open.

CHAPTER

— 11 —

Garen and I followed Father to the castle. I was so glad that Father had turned back into a human. We had spent nearly an hour sitting and hugging and crying to each other. When we finally released each other, Father helped me up.

"We need to get to your mother."

I nodded, and we started off. From where Father crashed as a Griffin, it was about a ten-minute walk from the castle. In no time at all, we were at the edge of the moat.

Father stopped where the drawbridge would come down and called out, "Captain Fedren!"

A minute or two later, I spotted Captain Fedren looking over the battlement. His eyes widened at the sight of Father. "Your Majesty! You're back early!" He turned around and I heard him call down into the courtyard, "Open the gate! The king is here!"

No sooner had the drawbridge lowered than we began the run across it. The huge doors swung open, and we ran in. The guards in the courtyard suddenly stopped and stared. I glanced at them and gave them a concerned look. What was wrong with my father coming back?

"Your Majesty!" Fedren called out as he descended the wall.

Father slowed down to a quick walk but did not stop. Fedren ran to catch up to him.

"Your Majesty, what are you doing back so soon? Renon said you wouldn't be back for a—"

I frowned. That was why the guards were surprised.

"Not now, Fedren. Not now ... Keep everyone away from the central tower. I don't know what could happen."

Father led the way to the tower, and Garen and I followed. Father's pace quickened. His strides lengthened, and Garen was able to match it. I, on the other hand, had to run to keep up. Father, I could tell, was agitated, and the more we walked, the more unsettled he grew. We passed more doors and went up at least two sets of stairs. I prayed that the Lord would help us and keep us safe as we began walking down a short corridor. It led to the staircase of the tower I had never been in. Father grabbed a torch near the staircase and began to ascend.

As we climbed up, I became winded. Father and Garen were taking the steps two at a time. The tower stairs spiraled on forever, and my breathing became labored. Not long after, we reached a landing with a ladder up to the trap door. The floor of the tower nearly brushed Father's head. He set the torch in a wall bracket and reached for the latch. It was bolted. Just before he touched it, it slid out of the lock. Father paused and then began to push on the door. Thunder suddenly sounded in the room above us, and we all fell to the floor of the landing.

"Garen, hand me your sword. I don't have mine on me," Father said, standing up. Garen unsheathed his sword and tossed it to him. Father again reached for the trapdoor. He thrust it open

"Harold!"

I looked up and gasped in delight. Leaning over the trapdoor was Mother. "Mother!" I called.

"Annabell!" Father rushed up the ladder and into the room. I quickly followed, with Garen on my heels. Entering the tower, I saw a gold sphere around us and Renon on the opposite side of it.

I glared at him. "You traitor!"

"Your Highness!"

I turned and gasped. Vermue was there, and he was the one who was making the sphere. I stared at him

"What ... how ... how did you get...?" I trailed off. He was still wearing the white robe we had first seen him in. He was wearing the same colors that William was. I pointed, wide eyed.

"You were William?"

He nodded, both hands still in the air, and turned to Father, who was staring at him wide eyed as well.

"Your Majesty, you need to take them and leave." His voice was strained, and his hands were starting to shake. "I have to destroy my brother's power. I can't hold this shield forever. You must hurry."

"He's your brother?" Garen said, pointing to Renon with an eighteen-inch dagger he had pulled out of his belt. Vermue nodded again, and his hands began to shake violently. The sphere began to ripple. Renon laughed.

"You won't be able to hold that for much longer, brother. You will never be able to protect them!" Renon yelled and started to fire spells. He shot mist and black bolts of lightning shot at the sphere. It struck the side of the sphere, pushing it in a few feet, but the side again smoothed out and hurled the bolt back toward him. He howled in rage as he dodged his own spells. The sphere shrank some. Vermue turned to Father again, his entire arm now shaking and his breath labored.

"Please Your Majesty, Leave quickly! As long as the sphere covers ... the door, you can't ... be hit."

Father quickly ushered Mother and me back down through the trapdoor. The sphere started shrinking again, and Lord Vermue let out a strained cry. I looked back and saw Garen run for the opening, but he wasn't quick enough. The shield receded over the trapdoor just as Garen was within a foot of it.

"Garen!" I yelled, but Father pulled me down and closed the door just as Renon shot a bolt of light on it. I looked up at it in fear. The bolt again slid back into the lock with a click. I grabbed the bolt and tried to shake it loose.

Father grabbed my hand, "Annabell, stop. We can't help Garen."

I turned to him. There were tears in his eyes. My hand dropped from the bolt, and I stood there looking up at it. Garen was where I couldn't help him. My breath came out shaky as I looked at both my parents

"We need ... need to pray."

Garen stared as the light hit the door. Renon laughed.

"It's locked now. There is no way for you to get out!" Garen frowned at Renon and transferred the dagger to his other hand. He knew that the sphere would at one point collapse, and both he and Vermue would be exposed to Renon's spells. He didn't dare step out of the dome until he absolutely had to. The sphere was still shrinking. Glaring at Renon, he stood in front of Lord Vermue. If he had to, he would fight Renon with his dagger. Garen didn't know what Renon would do to Vermue, but if Vermue couldn't keep the shield up, Garen would try to protect them both. He knew he might fail, but losing his life defending the royal family, and seeing God soon after, sounded better than doing nothing to stop Renon.

"Prepare to defend yourself," Garen said, again pointing the dagger at Renon. He gave a malicious laugh and reached into his pocket.

"So you think. You will never get me!" Renon yelled and tossed red powder into the air. It seemed to disintegrate, but when he began moving his hands in a circle, a red mist surrounded the dome.

"You need … to get behind me. He's shrinking the sphere. I am … going to try something." Lord Vermue's hands were shaking so hard they looked like they were vibrating. Garen, with his eyes still trained on Renon, stepped behind Vermue. He put the dagger back in his belt and grabbed Vermue's hands to steady them,

"How are you going to stop him? How can you?" Vermue turned and gave him a grateful look.

"Just stay behind me. You'll see."

"What's the matter, Vermue? Are you getting rusty, dear brother? Or just old?" Renon mocked him.

He began to spin his hands faster. A vortex began spinning around the sphere, causing it to move in on itself. The space around Garen and Vermue shrank. Renon stepped closer, his hands still spinning. The vortex's speed increased, and the sphere shrank some more.

"Do you really think you can do this? Was I not always better at things than you?" he said, glaring at Vermue.

Renon again stepped closer, and the sphere got too small to move around in.

"This is just what I wanted. Renon has been better at things than I have, but he isn't always wise," Vermue said, a pleased look crossing his face. He glanced at Garen.

"When I say three, let go of my arms."

Garen stared at him in shock. A few minutes ago, Lord Vermue's arms would have dropped if he had not held them up. Now he was asked to let them go? Garen looked at him again and saw that in Vermue's eyes that he had a plan. Garen gave him a nod as Renon took another step,

"Do you really think you can defeat—"

Vermue counted under his breath. "One … two … three!" Garen let go of his arms. They dropped, and the sphere disappeared. Instantly, Vermue created a white mist that enveloped both of them. Renon's vortex came to a halt as he froze, startled. This gave Vermue time to create another spell. A white bolt of light lit up the cloud, and Garen dropped to the floor in shock. Lightning flashed out of the cloud and struck Renon with such force that it knocked him off his feet and threw him into the stacks of boxes on the other side of the room. A thunderclap filled the room and shook the very tower itself.

"nooo!" Renon hit the crates and the pile fell on top of him. It was silent. Garen, still in the white mist, stayed on the ground, his breathing heavy. The white mist cleared and light filled the room. It seemed as if the sun itself had come in. Garen stood, covering his eyes, and called out to Vermue

"What's happening?"

"When the light fades, his power and knowledge of wizardry will go with it."

"How? That doesn't make any sense!" Garen tried opening his eyes but had to shut them again. The light faded, and Garen uncovered his eyes, blinking. He looked around the room and his gaze locked on Renon. He was slumped up against the boxes and crates, with a few on top of his torso and legs. His head had lolled to the side, and his eyes were closed. He had been knocked out. Garen turned to Lord Vermue and asked his question again.

"How can his power and knowledge of wizardry be gone?" Vermue looked at Renon, massaging his arms and hands from the ache of holding the sphere for so long,

"It's what happens when two wizards from the same family fling spells at each other. His spells didn't have an effect on me because of the sphere. When the spell, no matter what it is supposed to cause, hits or touches them, it makes their power disappear, along with their knowledge of how they became a wizard. It prevents them from becoming one again."

Renon began to moan and shift. Garen jumped and grabbed his dagger. Lord Vermue crossed the room, and Renon opened his eyes. Vermue helped him up out of the boxes and crates. Renon was still muddled and was shaking his head, trying to clear it. Garen looked at him cautiously and slowly slipped the dagger back into his belt.

"So he can't do anything anymore?"

Vermue shook his head. A rattling noise filled the room. The trapdoor began to shake and then sprang open with a loud *thud*.

I waited. I had prayed, my parents had prayed. Fear and what-if's kept running through my mind, and each time they did, I would pray again. Fifteen minutes passed in silence, and then above our heads, we heard the sound of the wind. We all looked up at the door. What was going on? I started for the ladder, and Mother grabbed my shoulder

"Don't." I looked at her, pleading, but she shook her head, fear still prominent in her eyes. I stared hard at the door. The wind sound grew louder, and then … it stopped. I looked wide eyed at my parents. What had happened? Suddenly the tower swayed, and thunder exploded above our heads. All three of us fell over at the sound. I stared up at the door again, my breathing shaky. Silence followed. A minute. Now two … three. All the silence was killing me. I stood up and turned to Father.

"I have to look. I need to help him!"

"Annabell, don't—" Voices sounded overhead and the bolt slid out of the lock.

I turned to Father again. "I have to look!"

I quickly reached up and grabbed the door's latch. I came up through the floor and looked around, worried. Father called from below for me to come back, but I ignored him. I found Garen standing facing Vermue and Renon, who looked rather disheveled and confused.

"Garen! Are you all right?" I rushed to his side and then looked around the room. The only thing that seemed to be ruined was the stack of boxes in the corner, and Renon, who was holding his head and moaning. I looked at Garen and, when I saw no injuries, was utterly relieved that nothing had happened to him. I gave him a hug.

At this, my tutor would have been shocked because "it isn't proper." But I didn't care. I released him from my hug and ran over to the trapdoor. I glanced over at Renon, who was still holding his head and leaning on Vermue's arm.

"It's all right, Father. They've stopped. You can come up."

Slowly, Father climbed up the ladder, with Mother right behind him. Now that Vermue wasn't holding up a sphere, he bowed to Father and Mother.

"Your Majesties, I would like to apologize for my brother's behavior. I had no idea he would do such a thing."

Father's temper and agitation had subsided when he saw Mother, but I could tell that he was still slightly upset with Renon.

"I accept your apology, Lord Vermue. What happened here?" he asked, looking at the boxes and then giving Renon a frown.

Vermue, who was still holding on to Renon's forearm, explained, "I've immobilized his power, Your Majesty. He can no longer perform any acts of wizardry."

Renon looked rather confused and rubbed his head, as if he was trying to remember what happened

Father glanced at him with a look of uncertainty, but then he crossed the room and laid his hand on Renon's shoulder. Renon lifted his head. "I forgive you, Renon."

I glanced at Father's face. There was a peace in his eyes and a sincerity in his speech. I let out a breath of air. Father had forgiven Renon. I had too. Even with all the trouble he caused, I forgave him. I realized that God had given my father unfathomable peace and that he had moved my father's heart to truly forgive him. I felt that peace in my spirit now too. I praised God and again forgave Renon.

Father looked at Lord Vermue. "Thank you, Lord Vermue, for saving us twice. How can I repay you?"

"There is no need, sire. I will be taking Renon back to Fizenburg with me. He no longer can be a wizard and will never threaten Misby again," he said, bowing.

Mother smiled and took Father's hand. "Thank you again. Are you sure there is nothing we can do for you?"

Vermue shook his head. "No, it is quite all right. It was my pleasure to assist you in finding Her Majesty. But now I must bid you farewell." And with that, he and Renon vanished in a puff of smoke.

EPILOGUE

The warm summer sun shone through the grand hall doors. It had been a month since Lord Vermue had left with Renon. My parents had given me a new owl to replace William. A normal owl that didn't talk and wasn't a wizard. Things had gone almost back to normal. Everyone in the palace now knew that I had the ability to talk to animals and other creatures. When animals weren't cooperating, servants or guards would come calling for my help. As for the advisor position, which had been opened since Vermue left with Renon. With Renon gone, Father needed a new advisor. Garen had been appointed to his place. Father appreciated his help so much that he gave him the task.

Garen fit right in with the position and was now around all the time. I was glad that with this change, I could visit him more often. My favorite change, though, had been that Mother and Father would not be traveling anytime soon. In the past month, I had spent more time with them than I thought possible, and I was very pleased about it. They had no desire to travel for a long while.

I walked up to my father's side. "God has met our needs, Father." He reached over and pulled me into a hug.

"He did, my daughter, and he does."

I let out a sigh of delight and stood there in my father's arms. We walked out the doors of the grand hall into the wonderfully warm sun, and I saw Garen. I left Father's side and went to Garen's side. He looked much different wearing a light-green shirt, embroidered sky-blue tunic, and the silver advisor's chain around his neck. He was standing there in the sun, praying.

"God answered our prayers, didn't he?"

Garen looked at me and smiled. "Yes, he has. He answers prayers all the time."

I gently nudged his side. "So how is your fear of heights now?" I said with a smile.

He smiled back. "Oh, I think it's gone, Your Highness."

Suddenly the alarm in the east guard tower rang. Garen and I looked up into the sky as Father and Mother came out.

A midnight-black creature flew into the courtyard and called out, "Where is Her Highness, Princess Annabell? I must speak with her! I have been sent from the Southern Continent." Of course, no one else could understand the creature but me. The creature landed in the courtyard, and this time no one attacked it. I walked up to it, my hand slightly raised.

"I'm Princess Annabell."

The creature inclined its horse-like head, "Your Highness, I have been sent to give you this message." In its claw was a letter. The creature handed the letter to me and then turned and flew away.

As I opened the message, Father, Mother, and Garen crowded around me.

I read the message:

> *Greetings to Your Highness,*
>
> *It has recently been spread that you are of the ability to talk to animals and the like. A recent disruption on the Central Continent is in dire need of your talent. A villain of unspeakable evil is at this moment destroying the safety of the kingdoms and continents as we know it. Your assistance is vital, with the help of others I am sending as well. All of you must work together and, in time, will meet me as well. I cannot*

tell you my exact location or who I am as it would put you and me in jeopardy. Please go at once to the Central Continent.

Your faithful servant

I looked at Father and gave him a half smile, "Here we go again."